'Firstly, don't call me Sandro. I don't like it.'

'But I thought you liked it before, when we were—'

Isandro laughed harshly. 'Before you deserted this marriage? Before you walked away from Zac? Well, that was then; this is now.'

Familiar pain lashed Rowan inwardly. 'But what about...what about what just happened...?' She hated the uncertainty in her voice, and was scrabbling to find covers to pull around her in protection.

Isandro started to walk away, his tall, lean and powerful body a vision in perfection. Gleaming golden skin stretched over hard muscles. He turned at the door.

'That's the second thing. We just slept together, that's all. It means nothing. And Rowan?' He didn't wait for an answer. 'This time I'll expect you to be willing when I want you, for however long I want you. Perhaps you'll be a better mistress than you were a wife.'

Abby Green worked for twelve years in the film industry. The glamour of four a.m. starts, dealing with precious egos, the mucky fields, driving rain…all became too much. After stumbling across a guide to writing romance, she took it as a sign and saw her way out, capitalising on her long-time love for romance books. Now she is very happy to sit in her nice warm house while others are out in the rain and muck! She lives and works in Dublin.

THE SPANIARD'S MARRIAGE BARGAIN

BY
ABBY GREEN

MILLS & BOON®
Pure reading pleasure™

First published in Great Britain 2008
Harlequin Mills & Boon Limited,
Eton House, 18-24 Paradise Road, Richmond, Surrey TW9 1SR

© Abby Green 2008

ISBN: 978 0 263 86468 7

Set in Times Roman 10½ on 12 pt
01-1008-54218

Printed and bound in Spain
by Litografia Rosés, S.A., Barcelona

THE SPANIARD'S MARRIAGE BARGAIN

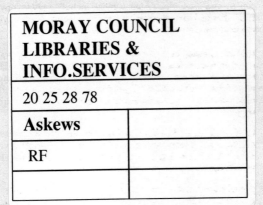

This is for Dr Larry Bacon, Dr Louise Campbell and Dr Jim Holden, with much thanks.

This is also especially for The Inspiring Ladies of the fledgling Women's Writers Circle in Scariff in County Clare, and even more especially for Ruth McMahon—who is soul sister, friend, guru and wise woman.

CHAPTER ONE

ROWAN CARMICHAEL faltered slightly as she stepped into the minimalist lobby of the small boutique hotel. She hadn't realised it was so exclusive. Even though she was well dressed, well enough to look as if she belonged here, she felt as though everyone must surely be able to see under her skin to the very heart of her, that beat so unsteadily. It had been so long since she'd been in a place like this. Another lifetime, another woman. She should have picked a more down-at-heel hotel. This kind of hushed luxuriousness reminded her of too much and made the skin on the back of her neck prickle.

She was completely oblivious to the several appreciative looks she drew, with her dark red hair and flawless creamy skin, which contrasted with her ever so slightly awkward grace as she moved.

Her expressive full mouth tightened as she looked for a seat, willing herself not to let the rising panic overwhelm her. She couldn't think of the past now. It was gone, and with it— Her step faltered again as a slicing pain ripped through her, stunning her with its intensity, with its rawness, its newness… even though it was old. And she felt old—a lot older than her twenty-seven years.

She found an empty seat and sank into gratefully. Within

moments a waiter had come to take her order for Earl Grey tea. She sat back and crossed her legs, taking a deep breath. She had to get it together. Had to be in control and above all *calm*.

She would have to discuss with a solicitor in less than ten minutes how she could best contact the husband she'd walked away from two years ago…and her baby. That slicing pain gripped her again, and she was made aware of how tenuous her control was. She needed time to gather herself. Perhaps she'd been silly, scheduling the appointment so soon; she was literally just off the train. This was the first time she'd been out in public again in two years. In the busy, heaving metropolis of London. Somewhere she'd truly never expected to be ever again.

No. She couldn't think like that. She'd be fine. After all, hadn't she been through so much worse?

This was the first day of the rest of her life. A new page, a new chapter.

A new beginning. And perhaps… A tiny alien bird of hope fluttered in her chest. Perhaps another chance at happiness? Even though in truth she'd had precious little happiness in her life so far…

Just then her attention was taken by a little boy, who was running and fell headlong at her feet on the marble floor. With instinctive and unquestioning swiftness Rowan was out of her seat and bending to lift the boy gently, her hands under his arms, a reassuring smile on her face.

'It's okay, sweetheart. I don't think you've really hurt yourself, have you? You look like a very brave boy.'

He stood unsteadily on chubby legs, his face veering between crying and not crying, a lip wobbling. He was adorable. Dark blond hair, olive skin and huge eyes…they were the colour of violets. Unusual and distinctive.

Too unusual and distinctive.

Shock slammed into Rowan like a punch in the gut. They were, in fact, the exact unique shade of violet that looked back at her in her own mirror every day. With that thought came a surge of something so instinctive, so primal, *so inexplicable* Rowan felt the world flip over and right itself again at an angle.

She held onto the boy. He'd obviously decided against crying, and looked at her guilelessly, his mouth cracking into a huge grin, showing tiny baby teeth. He rubbed his forehead and babbled something unintelligible, but she didn't hear him. The shock was so intense that she couldn't breathe.

This couldn't be him…*couldn't* be.

Had she dreamt of this moment for so long that she was hallucinating?

That was it. And perhaps arriving back like this was too much. Perhaps… But as she looked into his face, those eyes, she knew rationally it couldn't be possible. Yet her heart told another story, every instinct clamouring loudly.

She started to feel slightly desperate. Was this going to happen every time she saw a boy his age? Surely someone had to see her, had to *know*? Had to take him away from her—because she didn't think she would be able to move ever again. Or let him go.

Black-shod feet had appeared behind the boy. A man. There was a blur of movement and she had a sense of his size, his magnetism, even just in that quick moment as he bent down to pick the little boy up. His scent washed over her. *It was familiar.* Her heart had already stopped beating. Blood froze in her veins. Her hands dropped.

A coolly cultivated deep voice came from far above her head. The man spoke with a slight accent that was barely noticeable '…need eyes in the back of your head, they move so fast…'

She couldn't believe what she was hearing, or seeing. He

was tall, so tall that even when Rowan stood fully—she didn't know *how*—he towered over her own not inconsiderable height. He was so sinfully handsome that her brain seized—exactly the way it had when she had seen him for the first time.

Nearly three years ago.

This couldn't be happening. This was too, too cruel. Life *couldn't* be this harsh. And yet she knew well that it could.

He was still talking. And then abruptly he stopped, and the warm smile faded. Dark blond brows drew together over piercingly light blue eyes. The colour of blue ice. They pierced all the way through to Rowan's heart and soul, ripping her open, laying her bare to the myriad expressions crossing his face: the shock of recognition, disbelief…and then something much more potent. Disgust, anger…hatred. *Rejection.*

Rowan felt her mouth move as if to speak. But nothing came out. Everything seemed to hurtle around them in fast forward, but they were cocooned in an invisible bubble. Suspended in time. She looked at the little boy held high in his arms, and that was her downfall. She felt as if her heart would explode. It was all too much. She had one coherent thought before she slid into a dead faint at her husband's feet: *my baby.*

Isandro Vicario Salazar stood at the window of the bedroom in the suite that he'd carried Rowan upstairs to just a short time before. He looked at the distinctive telecom tower in the near distance, the bumper-to-bumper traffic in the streets down below, and saw none of it. His eyes were narrowed.

Rowan Carmichael. Rowan Salazar. His wife.

His mouth twisted into an even thinner line. His *errant* wife. The wife who had walked out on him and abandoned her own baby just hours after the birth because *she hadn't been ready to deal with it.* A drumbeat of rage, barely contained, beat under the surface of his skin. In his blood.

Stunning him with its force. That day he'd left her to rest after the birth, and returned some hours later—only to find her gone. He'd not laid eyes on her from that moment to this. He still reeled with the shock of seeing her. He reeled with the torrent of emotions that seeing her had evoked within him— emotions he'd suppressed long ago, *that day*, when she'd revealed her true nature and had shown him how unbelievably duped he had allowed himself to become. But not a hint of his inner emotions showed on his face even now.

A faint sound from the bed made him tense, and slowly he turned around.

Rowan waited a moment before opening her eyes. It was something she'd got used to in the past couple of years. A moment before reality rushed in, a moment to take stock, do a body-check, feel the sensations, feel if there was pain present…feel if she was *well*. But this time, as the muted sounds of car horns and traffic came from just outside, albeit a long way down, she tensed. The previous moments rushed back. The last thing she cared about right now was physical pain or if she felt well.

Her eyes flew open and there he was. It hadn't been a mirage. Her husband stood with his back to the window, hands deep in pockets of what she knew would be superbly crafted bespoke Italian cloth. Like his shirt and his jacket. The clothes moulded to his form, hugging every hard contour, em- phasising every part of his tall, broad-shouldered and powerful body. Exactly how she remembered…but even more devastating in the flesh.

She knew on some level that it was the cushion of shock that allowed her to be so coolly objective. He was, if anything, even more handsome. Although in fairness handsome was too trite a word, too *pretty*. He was altogether too male for a word like handsome. And he was right here in front of her, living, breathing…not a figment of her imagination. The exquisite pain of seeing him again when she knew well what he must think of her was mercifully not allowed to penetrate too deeply.

'So…' he drawled with a sardonic edge, 'you were obviously shocked to run into me. Surprising, really, considering this is my hotel.'

Rowan felt the numbness fade, the protective shock starting to shatter. *His hotel?* Since when had he owned a hotel in London? Even though he'd had to do a lot of business here, he'd never hidden his antipathy for the place. And how had she unwittingly chosen this hotel…out of a million others?

She'd quite literally come back and walked directly into the lion's den—like an industrious ant following the scent of a familiar pheromone.

How had she got up here to this room?

And then she remembered. It was too joyful and painful to bear, slicing through the shock and opening a raw wound. Her baby, her son…she'd seen him, held him. It *had* been him. She hadn't conjured him up. That knowledge was still too much for her to cope with fully; she knew that. Her brain would be close to going into meltdown if she focused on what had just happened too intensely.

'Did I…did I frighten him?' Her voice felt scratchy.

The cold flash of sheer disgust that crossed her husband's face was like a slap. If she'd had any doubts about his reaction they were laughably quashed now.

'No. If you had I wouldn't be here right now.'

The protective tone in his voice was unmistakable. Rowan pushed herself up to sit on the side of the bed. Her head still felt light, as if stuffed with cotton wool. Warily she looked up at Isandro. It almost physically hurt to see him like this after all this time. She'd dreamed of this moment for so long…but of course she had to concede that never in her imaginings had she fooled herself into believing that Isandro would be pleased to see her. That had been confined to her fantasies.

'Did you call him Zacarías?' she asked with a husky catch. Her eye was drawn to a muscle clenching in his jaw. But his curt, tight voice brought her eyes back to his.

'Zac. Yes.'

'After your grandfather…'

A look of disdain flashed across his face. 'Please let's not pretend that you actually care.'

Rowan winced, her face paling. She'd known exactly what she might expect when she confronted Isandro, but she just hadn't expected it so soon. She'd wanted to be in control, to have the chance to explain, be ready… Who was she kidding? In that moment she felt like she'd never be ready to explain.

'Your lover was sent on his way.'

Rowan had been in the act of standing, and promptly sat back down again. Isandro watched her coolly, but he felt anything but cool inside. It was taking all his self-control not to walk over, haul her up and demand…*what*? He shook inwardly with the force of the emotions running through him. The strongest of which felt suspiciously and awfully like jealousy. But he told himself it was only his pride that he cared about, that this vortex threatening to consume him couldn't possibly be linked into *feelings*. He'd learnt that lesson two years ago.

'My what?' She looked at Isandro incredulously. Now she really felt removed from reality.

'Your lover,' he spat out. 'The man you had come to meet. No doubt you have a room booked here somewhere? Is this how you've spent the last couple of years? In a debauched world tour of hotel rooms with insignificant men? Is this what you meant when you said you weren't *ready* to deal with marriage and motherhood?'

Insignificant men?

Rowan's head throbbed, and she put a hand to her temple, struggling to make sense of what he said. And then it hit her as a benign, friendly face swam into her mind's eye. She looked up at him again, her eyes wide. 'You must be talking about David Fairclough. He's my solicitor. I was due to meet him downstairs, just when…just when…'

Isandro snorted contemptuously. 'A likely story. You really wanted to rub my nose in it, didn't you?'

Rowan barely heard what he was saying. She finally found the strength to stand, her hands balled into fists at her sides. 'It is true. I was meeting him…' She faltered. She really hadn't planned on it happening this way, but there was nothing she could do now. She hitched up her chin. 'I was meeting him to discuss how best to contact you and talk about seeing my son.'

Isandro crossed his arms across his chest, making him look even more powerful, formidable. He blocked the light coming in from the window behind him and it made a shiver run down Rowan's spine.

'I can tell you right now that that is *not* going to happen.' His whole stance screamed rejection of her claim.

Panic coursed through Rowan. She stepped forward jerkily. 'But I have a right to see my child, no matter what's happened. You can't stop me.' To her utter chagrin her throat tightened with tears. She fought to control herself. She couldn't fall apart—not here, like this. She needed to be strong.

'I can and I will.' Isandro was icy and controlled. She shook her head and opened her mouth to speak, but he cut in ruthlessly. 'I wouldn't be surprised if you'd forgotten till today that it was a boy you had, you left so fast.'

Rowan's mouth closed, and the pain that lanced through her was raw and overwhelming. Her voice sounded thready to her ears. 'I… Of course I knew he was a boy. I've thought of nothing else but him every day since—'

Isandro took two quick strides and gripped Rowan's arm painfully. 'Enough!'

She took a sharp breath to disguise the pain. This was far worse than she had anticipated. She couldn't afford to forget that this man wielded a power that was on a par with the world's most prominent politicians. Would telling him what had really happened make him see…make him understand? She'd hoped it would, with the cushion of distance between them. The lingering rawness made her feel as though a layer of skin had been stripped from her body. The truth would lay her bare completely, but right now, having met her son when she'd truly believed she'd never see him again, shock was making her reckless.

'Isandro. Please, I can tell you what happened. Maybe then you'll understand—'

He cut her off harshly. 'Understand? *Understand?*'

His face was so close that she could see the fine lines spreading from the corners of his eyes, could see his skin, golden and taut over those high cheekbones. She held herself rigid, would not give in to her body's demand to allow herself to really acknowledge what his proximity was doing to her. How could she when he was looking at her with such unbridled hatred, making her feel confused and inarticulate?

Scorn dripped from every syllable of his every word. 'I know what happened. You left a note…remember? There is not one thing, not one word, not one lame story you could dream up to excuse what you did that day. You took away an innocent baby's most important source of nourishment and love. Security. There is no one and nothing on the planet that could absolve you of that crime. You gave up your right to be a mother to him when you walked away, just hours after he was born.'

And you gave up the right to be my wife...

The words, unspoken, hung heavy in the air.

Rowan's inarticulate explanation died on her lips. His stark, cruel words resounded in her head. For a short, bliss-fully deceptive moment she felt no reaction to them, was numbed, and then like poison-tipped arrows they joined with the ever-present debilitating guilt and sank deep, deep into her heart, robbing her of words, of any explanation she might give.

He was right. She couldn't say a word. Not right now anyway. How could she expect him to understand that which she had barely come to terms with herself? That which she'd only just very painfully started to forgive herself for? She *had* walked away from her own newborn baby. Had she really thought that telling him her reasons might absolve her? She didn't deserve that.

Her control was close to breaking, but she knew she couldn't afford to crumble now. She had to face the conse-quences of her actions, not seek absolution. She dredged up some much needed strength and pulled away from his iron grip jerkily.

Isandro watched her dispassionately. She backed away farther, her hand going to rub her arm where he had gripped it. His anger was cooling to a contained icy rage. She turned away for a moment, offering him her back, and his eyes flicked down. In her smart suit and high-necked blouse he could see for the first time that she was slimmer than she had been. The short jacket and straight skirt didn't hide much. Desire burned low and insistent in his belly, even though everything in him rebelled at his unwanted response. She'd always been slim, but there was an unmistakable fragility to the lines of her body now that hadn't been there before.

He hated to think it, and quashed it almost immediately, but was there also a *vulnerability*? Her Titian hair had been long before, down her back, but now it was much shorter, exposing the line of her elegant neck. She still had that quintessential upper class deportment that couldn't be faked. She'd been his access into a world notoriously hard to break into for outsiders: the upper echelons of the English banking system, an ancient and tightly guarded group of the super-wealthy elite.

With what had been an extremely uncharacteristic failing to read another person, she had been the first person *ever* he'd so badly misjudged. Monumentally. Catastrophically.

She turned around to face him again and her eyes were flashing, taking him by surprise. But then his resolve hardened. *This* was the real woman he had married. But unaccountably, even as he thought that, his eye was involuntarily drawn to the crest of her breasts, pushing against the fine silk of the blouse. He felt his body tighten even more in response to their fullness, felt sensual tension flooding his veins. His reaction was so unwarranted that it momentarily stunned him. And then she spoke, cutting through the haze in his brain. He told himself it had to be shock.

'Whether you like it or not, I have rights. Any court in the world will recognise that. Whatever I did, I will be allowed to see my son. Eventually.' Her voice was clipped, her breeding coming through with every well-enunciated syllable, taking Isandro's mind off the unpalatable reactions in his body.

Rowan watched his reaction warily. He mustn't know what it was costing her to stand here and speak to him like this. She felt as if she was back in elocution class. But it was the only way she was clinging onto that flimsy control.

Isandro's face was a stony mask of non-reaction as he took her by surprise, starting to walk away. 'You will remain in this room for now. If you attempt to leave there is a bodyguard outside this door who will bring you back inside.' All he knew was that he had to put some distance between them, take stock of what had just happened.

Rowan watched incredulously as his long powerful strides took him towards the door. Belatedly she went after him, stumbling a little. 'Wait—where are you going? We haven't finished discussing this.'

He turned at the door and the cold force of his gaze stopped her in her tracks. 'Oh, yes—we have. For now. Just remember this: you deserted your son and left him with me. I can make this easy or very, very hard. It's up to you.'

When he opened the door, Rowan saw the great big hulking shape of a bodyguard just outside and heard a small voice chatter excitedly. 'Papa—Papa!'

The door closed and she felt the bed at the back of her legs behind her. Hearing that small voice was too much. Her legs crumpled and she slid to the ground. For a long time she sat like that, with her legs tucked under her, stunned by everything. It was only after a few minutes that she realised her cheeks were wet with tears, and she held a fist to her chest as if she could soothe the pain in her heart.

Eventually Rowan got up and went into the bathroom, where she splashed some water on her face. Towelling herself dry, she studied her reflection. Her face was white, her eyes huge. She looked and felt like a deer caught in the headlights. She needed to look in control, not half shocked out of her wits and terrified. Out of the corner of her eye she noticed her bag on the bed. Isandro must have picked it up from where it had fallen when she'd fainted. She wished she had some make-up, but she didn't have a thing—make-up had been the last thing on her mind for a long time.

She went back into the bedroom and tried pinching her cheeks to restore some colour. Standing at the window, looking out on the view that Isandro had seen only a short time before, she held her body tense. She still couldn't believe how the fates had brought them together. It was laughable. She'd chosen this hotel primarily because it was close to St Pancras, where she'd gotten off the train from Paris, and because her solicitor's office was uncomfortably close to Isandro's London offices. It had been under A on the internet, for Alhambra Hotel. But in the end she would have been safer meeting David Fairclough at his office.

She felt a fleeting moment of ironic humour. She'd counted on being able to gather all her information, had banked on the fact that Isandro would most likely be in Spain. They would contact him by letter to let him know of her wishes, her intentions to get to know her son… But instead here they were. The chance to explain in depth her reasons for leaving that day by the luxury of a letter was gone. Faced with Isandro's virulent anger, she knew he was in no mood to listen—possibly for some time. And now he believed that he'd caught her in the midst of an afternoon tryst. The worst possible start to any kind of meeting.

And then there was her son. Her baby. *Zac*. He was so beautiful. Rowan put a hand to the curtain, gripping it tight as she felt weakness flood her, her legs turning to jelly.

Meeting Isandro again was something she'd been somewhat prepared for. But how did you prepare to meet the child you thought you'd never see ever again? Every step of that walk away from him was etched into her memory like a searing brand. She'd woken from nightmares reliving that walk almost every night for the past two years. Her bruised and battered heart beat unsteadily against her chest. That indescribable pain and the lingering joy of seeing him all swirled together, making her feel like crying and laughing at the same time.

Rowan heard the door open behind her. Her hand tightened on the curtain before she released it from her grip. She took a deep breath and turned around. Isandro. His face was so harsh and austere that Rowan sucked in a breath. He *hated* her. She could feel it tangibly as he came and stood in front of her, head back, looking down at her with heavy-lidded disgust. His blue eyes were like shards of ice.

'I have some business to attend to here in the hotel. You are by all means free to go if you wish.'

Her mind and heart seized in a painful spasm at his *volte face*. The thought of being so close to her son and being sent away now was wrenching and unbearable.

'No.' She shook her head. 'I'm not going anywhere. I came back to London to get in touch with you. Believe what you want, but I had no idea you owned this hotel. I'm not leaving now until you agree for me to see Zac.'

His mouth tightened with unmistakable displeasure. He obviously hadn't expected that. But there was also something she couldn't put her finger on. A hint of resignation? Did he realise that he couldn't just dismiss her?

'Very well. In that case you will remain in this room tonight, and tomorrow morning we may discuss things.'

Rowan looked at him sceptically. She'd expected more of a fight. Why wasn't he flinging her out on the steps? He was playing with her, a master tactician.

'No need to look so suspicious, Rowan. You are, after all, my wife—are you not? Naturally I am overjoyed to see you again.'

With a mocking look on his face he backed away before

turning and leaving the room. When an outer door shut too, Rowan knew that she was finally quite alone. Hesitantly she opened the door into the outer part of the suite and looked around. Her suitcase had also been transported upstairs. Breathing a little easier for the first time in hours, Rowan went to a couch and sat down. Half distracted, she felt something underneath her and plucked it out. It was a furry toy animal.

Zac. With a shaking hand she brought it close to her face and breathed deep. The well of emotion was rising to consume her again and she couldn't keep it back. Clutching the small teddy, Rowan curled up on the couch and gave in to the storm.

Much later that night Isandro found himself at the door of the suite just down the hall from his own private rooms. What was he doing here? He opened the door and stepped in. The light was dim, the curtains still open, and it was only as he walked towards the bedroom that he saw the shape on the sofa.

His heart fell. Why couldn't she have just disappeared?

He knew damn well why.

She was back to get everything her greedy little hands could carry. No doubt including his son. Look at her. He almost laughed out loud when he saw Zac's toy clenched in one hand, close to her face. She'd come back from whatever rock she'd been hiding under, like an actress poised in the wings of the stage, ready to make her entrance.

Yet, much to his dismay, faced with her benign sleeping form, Isandro was helpless against a rush of memories. The first time he'd seen her across a packed function room where he'd come to meet Alistair Carmichael. Rowan's father had been a man in dire straits, about to become publicly bankrupt unless Isandro agreed to a mutually beneficial deal. Carmichael had known that Isandro wanted in, and Isandro had known Carmichael needed saving from public humiliation and ruination. In the middle of it all had been Rowan. Part of the deal.

He'd seen her across that crowded room and, like an old cliché, their eyes had met. He'd felt a little poleaxed by their intense shade of dark violet-blue, their seriousness, when so many women looked at him with another expression entirely.

She'd been unbelievably gauche-looking—too gauche, in fact, and he now knew for a fact that it had all been an act. Then he'd spotted her father by her side and he'd put two and two together. *This* was the daughter the old man wanted to marry off. Carmichael had baited him with the fact that if she married she'd come into her mother's sizeable inheritance.

He had let Carmichael believe that he might want a bride who came with a dowry, suspecting that the banker had designs on much of his daughter's inheritance himself. Isandro had had no need for the dowry, of course. But what he had needed, much more importantly, was another level of acceptance. Social acceptance. Without a *bona fide* English society wife, his taking control of Carmichael's chair at the bank would be for ever frowned upon. He'd be as socially ostracised as a beggar on the streets. However, if it was a merger of two great families—one Spanish, with links to the formidable banking industry there, the other English—then that was a different story. Acceptance would be immediate, and would consolidate his control over banking in Europe.

Which was exactly what had happened.

His mouth tightened in rejection of the way his thoughts seemed to be defying him, leading him back to a place he never wanted to visit again. What he hadn't counted on was the place that his meekly unassuming new wife would take in his life. And what it had done to him when he had discovered the true depth of her avaricious and shallow nature. What it had done to him to come back into that hospital room to find her gone. Leaving nothing but a note and her wedding rings. It had made him the biggest fool—because all along, right up until that moment, he'd believed her to be different.

He stepped noiselessly back out of the room and vowed with everything in his body that she would pay for her actions a million times over.

CHAPTER TWO

THE next morning Rowan sat tensely in a chair and watched the door of the suite. She'd woken early, to find herself stiff and uncomfortable on the couch, still holding Zac's toy. With the arrival of the morning things were clearer in her head. She could not let Isandro intimidate her. She had to make him see that she had rights. She cursed her own lack of foresight. Today was Saturday, and she didn't have her solicitor's home or mobile number. She should have rung him yesterday, after Isandro had left…but she'd been feeling so shocked. She knew that it was a mistake that could cost her dearly.

The truth was, she'd only contacted her solicitor in anticipation of the worst-case scenario—that Isandro, on being contacted, would prove intractable and unforgiving. She was still too much of a coward to admit to herself that she had harboured the wish that somehow, despite everything, once he knew, they could be a happy family. A hundred jeering voices mocked her naïve fantasy.

But they had been happy. They had had *something*. But, she had to concede painfully, that had been *before*, in the earlier months of their time together. Isandro had been the first man to draw Rowan out of herself, the first man she'd slept with…the first man she'd fallen for. He'd made her feel beautiful, desirable. And, to her shame, she found she was remembering that, and not her discovery of what he'd really felt for her: which was *nothing*.

That brought her mind back to reality. No doubt Isandro would already have consulted with an army of legal advisors on how best to deal with the reappearance of his wife. His ability to adapt and react to situations had always awed her. This would be no different. She could well imagine that David Fairclough would have been intimidated out of his skin yesterday, faced with Isandro's wrath.

Suddenly the door opened, taking her by surprise, and Rowan jerked up to stand, all of her clear-sightedness deserting her with the arrival of her husband. Her body was rigid with tension as she took in his dark blond good-looks, his hair slightly tousled, as if he'd been running a hand through it.

Isandro closed the door softly behind him, watching her. Her face was still as pale as alabaster, her eyes like two huge bruises of colour. His own eyes ran up and down her form. She trembled as lightly as a leaf, barely perceptible.

'I trust you slept well?' he asked innocuously, with no evidence of the will he was imposing onto his body's response to seeing her. Anger at this renewal of response surged through him.

'Very well. The bed was most comfortable.' Rowan was not going to pretend for a second that she hadn't had a night of perfect restful sleep.

A fleeting expression that she couldn't decipher crossed his face as he pushed away from the door and came close. Rowan fought against backing away.

This morning his jacket and tie were gone, shirtsleeves rolled up. She noticed what looked suspiciously like dried food on his shirt. Had he been feeding Zac? An overwhelming urge to see her son again nearly floored her. She needed to see that he was *real*, that she hadn't imagined him. That he was as beautiful and healthy as he'd looked…

Isandro folded his arms. Everything about him was forbidding. Rowan forced her swirling emotions down.

'Your timing is impeccable…but then I guess you've proved that already.'

Rowan's eyes met his cold ones. She ignored his barb. Waited to hear what he would no doubt explain. He brushed past her to the window, as if in deliberate provocation, and Rowan sucked in a betraying breath at the way he took her off guard by coming so close. At the way her skin prickled uncomfortably. His cool and musky scent wrapped around her, and another scent…that baby scent. Her heart lurched in reaction.

He stayed with his back to her for a moment. For some reason he couldn't trust himself to face her, and he hated that. He spoke in a monotone. 'Two months from now it will be two years exactly since you walked out of that hospital. You've returned now because we can both file for divorce and you can get your hands on the money agreed in the prenup. I see you've been careful not to go beyond the two-year desertion mark, which would have biased things against you. It must be killing you to come back and disrupt your *plans*, but once the divorce is through you'll be off again.' He turned around and fixed her with those laser eyes. 'Yes?'

Rowan struggled through waves of shock at his cool mention of divorce to understand what he'd said. She had no concept of time or legalities. She'd come here now because she was able. *Because she was finally well enough…*

His arms were folded, every line in his face regal, hard, uncompromising. Her betrayal and his own shaming lack of judgment seared him again now he was faced with her wide-eyed act of shock. He laughed briefly, harshly. 'Come now—even you, with all your guile, hardly expected us to play happy reunited families?'

Rowan shook her head. His words, which committed to dust that childish and secret fantasy, had rendered her momentarily speechless.

His voice assumed a bored tone which did even more damage to her heart. 'You've done me a favour. If you hadn't turned up now I wouldn't have been able to seek a divorce without your consent, so you've saved me the tedious job of having to track you down.' His expression changed in an instant, and he moved closer, looking at her assessingly. 'Let me guess. You've run out of your inheritance?'

Rowan blanched, going even paler. The sizeable inheritance from her mother *was* almost gone, but not for the reasons he'd so obviously guessed. But it was too late. He'd seen her reaction. A hard, triumphant glitter made his eyes icy.

'As I thought.' He shook his head. 'You know, it disappoints me how predictable you women are. But then I don't know why I'm surprised. I should have known this was on the cards.' He continued. 'So now you're back, seeking to cash in on a prenup which will give you a nice nest egg…although at the rate you got through your mother's money, I can't see that mine will last much longer.'

Rowan's anger built with a white-hot flash. She felt colour bloom in her cheeks and welcomed it. 'I have no desire for your money, Isandro. The only thing I desire is to see my son.'

He looked bored. 'I can see how he will be a good pawn for you, but please do not insult my intelligence. Turning up now shows just how deeply your mercenary streak runs. Being the mother of my son is an added insurance, to make sure you get as much as possible. No doubt this was all part of the grand plan.'

The grand plan? If only he knew…

'Tell me,' he said thoughtfully, 'have you already planned your public defence? Are you going to go with postnatal depression, which is what the papers hinted at as being the likely cause of your curious absence from my side?'

Her mouth fell open. 'Postnatal depression…you mean people don't know?' Rowan had feared that the press would have heard how she had deserted her child after she'd gone. She'd been prepared to deal with it, and it was more than surprising to her that Isandro hadn't leaked the news for maximum benefit… Yet how could she forget that towering Spanish pride?

Isandro's eyes narrowed on hers. 'Why are you doing this? Why are you pretending you don't know?'

'But… I don't…' Rowan felt woolly in the head. For the first six months after her departure she hadn't seen one newspaper. Or the news. And by the time she'd been exposed to it again she'd never seen any mention of Isandro. She'd fought the urge to go looking, because every time she felt it, the guilt would rise up and overwhelm her. Her husband was the type of man rarely mentioned in tabloids or the common press. His power and astronomical wealth were such that he was effectively removed from such banal speculation or scrutiny. Protected.

However, the papers must have read *something* into the fact that Isandro Vicario Salazar's wife had seemed to suddenly disappear from the face of the earth.

He answered her unspoken thoughts. 'Nobody is aware of the fact that you deserted this marriage. They lost interest when I returned to Spain with Zac, believing that you had simply taken refuge from prying eyes at our…*my* Seville home.'

Rowan struggled to take it all in. 'And your family…?' She

remembered his mother's austere and pain-lined face. The coolness with which she had endured the wedding in London, patently hating every minute of it. Rowan also remembered the equally cold and suspicious face of Isandro's older sister, Ana. Neither had offered any form of welcome.

'Oh, they know exactly what happened. Somehow they weren't surprised.'

Rowan knew she had to sit or else she'd fall. She walked unsteadily to a chair in the corner and sat down. She felt incredibly weary all of a sudden, and the magnitude of the fight she faced was sinking in. She couldn't let the stark reality that he fully expected them to divorce overwhelm her. He didn't have to know how little she'd prepared for this, and now she welcomed the prompt which had led her to seek a meeting with her solicitor.

'All I want is to be able to see my son. That's why I was meeting Mr Fairclough yesterday. Even I know that as Zac's mother I *will* be allowed see him.'

Isandro fought down the anger that rose when she mentioned Zac's name. He decided to go with his own plan and see how far he got. But he didn't doubt that Zac was the golden ticket in Rowan's plan.

'I can have divorce papers drawn up today.'

Rowan's heart sank. She was going to be faced with Isandro's full ammunition.

'If you agree to divorce proceedings, and agree to the terms I'll outline for granting you access to Zac, I'll triple the amount stipulated in the prenuptial agreement and it will be transferred into your account immediately.'

Rowan blanched. That sum of money would keep a small country running for some years. But she had no interest in money.

She stood up from her seat and raised her chin. She had to

be strong. She could crumble later. She had to focus on Zac, because to think of anything else right now was too much to bear. 'No.'

'No?' Isandro's face darkened with anger. He was caught in a bind and he had no doubt that she knew it.

'I'll agree to…to…' To her utter chagrin her mouth and tongue stumbled on the words. She felt herself flushing. 'To the divorce, by all means. It's not as if this marriage was ever a love-match. I'm well aware of that. But I will not put my name to anything that signs away my rights to Zac. Those are bullying tactics, Isandro, and I won't be bullied.' She folded her arms to conceal their shaking.

Isandro had to admit to feeling slightly flummoxed. He'd never been accused of being a bully before, and it didn't sit well with him. Bullies acted without intelligence, on frightened instinct, and he had to concede now that he *was* frightened. Frightened of what she could do to his son. Frightened of a lot more than he cared to name at the moment.

'He's my son. I carried him for almost nine months. I gave birth to him. You can't take that away from me. You can't—'

Isandro crushed the surprise he felt as she stood up to him so calmly. 'And yet despite all that you were able to walk away without even a backward glance.'

Rowan's throat closed over again. *She'd put her son first. If she had looked back then she'd never have left, and that would have meant…*

She stopped her painful thoughts with effort and controlled herself. 'I don't care about your money. I just want to know my son.'

Who was she kidding? He had to stop himself from laughing out loud. This was a woman who had married him to get her hands on her inheritance and had got pregnant in a calculated bid to extract as much money as she could from him. And here was the evidence. Right in front of him. She was wily and canny. He'd give her that. She knew exactly what she was doing by returning just before two years was up. It meant that any claim he made of desertion would be called into question, might be investigated. And even though he had the note she'd left as evidence, he knew that if she were conniving enough she could turn it around to work for her.

The sheer evidence of her premeditation stunned him anew. This wasn't the meek, shy wallflower he thought he'd married. She'd been a virgin on their wedding night! The ultimate in innocence and purity. She'd even maintained the façade right through her pregnancy— He halted his thoughts with effort and dug his hands deep in the pockets of his trousers, tightening the material across his groin. His shirt, open at the neck, hinted at the dark olive skin underneath, with crisp whorls of hair just visible.

For a second Isandro's physical presence hit Rowan hard between the eyes, and out of nowhere came a vivid memory of herself underneath him, his naked body pushing down over hers, chest to chest. She remembered taking him into her on a single breath, he'd thrust so deeply that she'd truly believed in that moment that he'd touched her heart.

She shook her head faintly, feeling acutely warm and breathless. The room—it must be the room. It was too hot, she told herself.

Isandro was speaking again. 'You leave me no option, then.'

'No option…?' she repeated stupidly fighting an urge to open her own shirt at the neck and let some air get to her skin. She was feeling constricted.

It utterly galled Isandro that even though she'd behaved reprehensibly as Zac's mother she *could* swan back onto the scene like this and have rights. Any court in the world would see the importance of a child being allowed to bond with its mother. His own lawyer had advocated that he should not be seen to stand in the way of reasonable access; it would only damage him down the line. As much as he wanted to turn around, walk away, forget she existed, he couldn't.

He didn't know why she wasn't taking the small fortune he was offering, but thought it could only be because she believed she'd get even more with this charade of belated concern. He had to be seen to give her a chance. But if he was going to do it then it would be on *his* terms, on *his* turf. He couldn't trust that if he left her behind now she wouldn't try and do something dramatic, using Zac in order to wage a public campaign for custody—and ultimately for the millions she no doubt craved.

'If you mean what you say about being here purely to see and get to know Zac, then you will return to Seville with us within the hour.'

His words cut through her body's inexplicable response. She focused on the clear blue of his eyes and felt as if they were impaling her. 'Go on.'

'You will come and live in my house for a sufficient amount of time to prove your…good intentions towards Zac. You will be allowed a certain amount of supervised access—'

'But—'

'But nothing. These are my terms, Rowan, and you're not in a position to argue.'

Rowan swallowed as she acknowledged her weak position. 'I told you—my only concern is being with Zac as much as I possibly can.'

'Well, then, you can't *possibly* have a problem with this.'

Living with him in his house…in such close proximity… her every move watched and monitored…

Rowan looked up at him. 'I…don't—I just…couldn't I stay somewhere nearby?'

Isandro waved an impatient hand. 'That is not practical. If you are serious about getting to know Zac it's best to see him in his own environment. I won't have you coming along, disrupting his routine, taking him out of his home. No way.'

Rowan wrung her hands. 'Of course I wouldn't do that. I didn't mean that, I just…'

'This is it, Rowan. Take it or leave it. You're hardly in a position to negotiate.'

He watched the turmoil in her eyes. No wonder she was balking at his suggestion. It proved how false her intentions really were. To go from two years of hedonistic freedom to being holed up in his home in a small town outside Seville—she'd be climbing the walls within weeks, if not days. Not to mention spending time with a small toddler who had the smile of an angel but who would test the patience of a saint.

'I'll give you five minutes to think about it.'

Rowan watched, still slightly dumbstruck, as he turned and left the room. The door shut softly behind him, the sound incongruous in a room heavy-laden with atmosphere and tension.

Rowan paced up and down. She had to think fast. Isandro was not used to having to wait for anything or anyone. She knew what she should do was stay in London, meet her solicitor and see what her options were. But that would be next week now. In the meantime this tenuous connection would be broken. Isandro would be back in Spain with Zac. And with his obvious determination to divorce, who knew how hard he'd prove to be to contact once the matter was in his legal team's hands? It could be months, even longer before she got to see Zac again. She had no doubt that Isandro would do whatever it took to make her look as bad as possible, and she had to concede that wouldn't be hard at all… How would it look if it emerged that she'd turned down an offer to go and live with her son?

Perhaps that was what he was hoping? That she would shoot herself in the foot…

She had to put aside her feelings for Isandro. Her one priority was Zac. When she'd seen him, touched him yesterday, she'd *known* him—incredibly. That primal recognition and joy struck her again.

This was the moment she had to let go of the fantasy. The wish that somehow something of *before* could be salvaged. She'd irretrievably damaged everything. Fate and circumstance had led her down a difficult path. And she had to remind herself that no matter what she'd led herself to believe, to hope for in their marriage, she'd been living in a fantasy all along anyway.

She firmed her mouth. Now was not the time to indulge in old memories. Once she'd unwittingly overheard that conversation with his sister well into her pregnancy she'd known exactly where she stood, how he felt. Their marriage obviously hadn't become for him what it had become for her, no matter what she'd thought at the time. *Or hoped…* She'd berated herself for her fanciful notions—what had she known, after all? She'd been a virgin when they'd first slept together. And he… She flushed hotly. Well, he certainly hadn't. She pressed cool hands against her cheeks to try and stem the heat.

Zac was here. She'd seen him. There was no way she could walk away again. She didn't have it in her. She didn't want to be miles away, not knowing, missing even more of his life. She would prove herself to her husband if it was the last thing she did. And then he would *have* to acknowledge her role in their son's life.

'Well?' Isandro stood at the door, dressed impeccably in jacket and tie again, every inch of him the banking giant whose influence induced fear and awe among adversaries and colleagues alike. Her eye caught that muscle twitching in his hard jaw. The fact that he wasn't as controlled as he looked was no comfort.

Rowan looked at him steadily and said, very clearly, 'I'm coming with you.'

After that things happened with scary swiftness. Isandro plucked a phone from his pocket and made a call, unleashing a stream of Spanish that Rowan only understood bits of. Her once fluent command of the language was rusty from lack of use.

He finished the conversation and pocketed the phone. He had an implacable expression on his face, but she could sense the underlying anger and impatience. He did not want her coming with him. She was quite sure that he had most likely been advised by someone that to offer to bring her back to Spain was a good idea. And he had expected her to say no. To be so unwelcome made her feel a little queasy.

'Where do we need to go to get your things?'

Rowan shook her head. 'Nowhere. I have everything with me.'

Isandro's body stilled. He flicked a derisive glance to the tiny case by her side. 'Everything?'

She nodded. 'It's all in there. And I have my passport in my handbag.'

'You haven't been living here?'

She shook her head, unbelievably stung by the evidence of his uninterest. He really had taken her note to heart. He hadn't tried to find her. And while that had been her objective in leaving the provocative note…it still *hurt*.

He took a step closer as he straightened his cuffs. 'Care to tell me where you *have* been living? Or do you expect me to believe you've been living out of a suitcase that size for two years?'

Rowan blinked and swallowed painfully. She had, actually.

If he looked hard enough he might recognise that it was the case she'd had with her in the hospital, when she'd given birth to Zac…might even recognise that this, her one and only decent suit, was also two years old. But of course he wouldn't. His questions were cutting far too close to the bone. Literally.

'It doesn't matter where I've been, Isandro. What matters is that I'm here now.'

His eyes were intensely blue on hers for a long moment. And then he shrugged. 'Come. It's time to leave.'

Rowan hitched her bag on her shoulder, and had caught the handle on her suitcase when he surprised her by coming back and leaning close, to take it out of her hand with a brusque movement. Their hands touched. She was so shocked at this contact that she snatched hers back, as if burnt. She could feel her eyes widening, her breath quicken, her heart race, and knew she looked shocked, but couldn't hide her response.

He stood to his full height and, helpless, Rowan could only gaze up into his eyes. That small physical contact was unleashing a maelstrom of sensations, images, memories, and, as if Isandro knew exactly what was going on inside her, he looked her up and down with studied insolence. His look, when it came to rest on her face again, was remote, utterly cold, and Rowan was in no doubt that he had just read her perfectly and did not welcome her reaction. Rejection flowed from every line of his tautly held body, and she had never felt so humiliated in her life.

By some small miracle he said nothing, merely turned on his heel, carrying the case and walked out of the room, not even checking to see if she was following. She caught up with him at the lift. He was staring resolutely ahead. She still burned.

'Where…?' She hated the tentative sound of her voice. 'Where is Zac?'

The bell pinged and she followed Isandro into the lift. He

waited till they were descending and said coolly, 'Zac has gone on ahead to the plane with his nanny. By the time we get there he should be down for his nap, so will have the minimum of disruption to his schedule.'

'Oh.' She was struck, heartened to see how closely attuned to his son's life he obviously was.

The lift doors pinged again and opened onto the lobby. Isandro strode out. Rowan struggled to keep up. A very attractive woman in a suit hurried over to speak to him, and when he stopped Rowan could see that she wore a manager's badge. She had huge blue eyes that looked up at Isandro with undisguised appreciation. He smiled down at her easily, and for a second Rowan couldn't breathe, such was the force of his smile. She'd forgotten just how potent his charm was. Not that he'd ever had to lavish much on *her*; she'd been a conquest he hadn't had to woo, after all.

The manager was speaking in an efficient yet slightly breathy tone that grated on Rowan's nerves. 'When we get that analysis report you requested I'll have it sent over to Spain immediately.'

'Thanks, Carrie.' Isandro started walking again, with the other woman beside him, effectively shutting Rowan out as if she didn't exist.

Then they were outside, where a sleek limousine was waiting with doors open. Isandro gestured for her to get in, careful not to touch her, Rowan noticed. When she sat in the car she was slightly out of breath. She watched as they pulled away from the hotel and eased into the morning traffic.

'I thought you hated London.' She could remember his irritation when business had kept him tied here after their perfunctory wedding, and then her advancing pregnancy which had precluded moving back to Spain until after the birth.

He flicked her a hard glance. 'I do.'

'So why this hotel?'

This time he did turn more fully, and settled back into the seat. Rowan instinctively inched back as far as she could.

'Why the interest, Rowan? Already adding it as a possible to the portfolio you're hoping to receive if the money's not enough? You should have taken me up on my first offer. It won't come around again.'

She decided to ignore that. 'I was just wondering, that was all.'

She faced the front. Isandro studied her profile, the straight nose, determined chin. Long sweep of black lashes. Surprisingly full lips…soft and inviting. He despised his unwarranted lack of control, over a woman so completely without morals, despised the fact his desire could not be governed by his intellect. Back in the suite just now, when she'd looked at him with such naked desire, for a second he'd actually forgotten just who she was and had felt his body quicken to a hot response. Exactly as she'd no doubt intended.

He forced his mind away from that. He needed words. To speak. Cut through the images…the memories.

'I bought the hotel after Zac was born. I can't ignore the fact that he's half-English. This is part of his heritage. It'll serve as an investment for him for the future, should he ever decide he wants to come here.'

Rowan didn't answer. She was too shocked by the tender feelings his words evoked, the memories of other times when she'd seen that tenderness come through. It had made her fall irrevocably in love with him, the contrast between hard-nosed ruthless businessman and his much more secret side. A side she thought only *she* had been privy to. A side that she had come to believe in—which she should *never* have believed in. She welcomed the hardness that settled around her heart. She had to protect herself. To remember.

She cast a quick glance at him. The aquiline line of his nose and full lips gave him a profile that spoke of sensual knowledge and promise. He gave no indication of knowing he was under scrutiny. Then his head turned and those eyes snagged hers. Dead on. Heat flared upwards from the pit of her belly and Rowan turned away. She could almost feel the mocking, knowing smile that curved his lips.

CHAPTER THREE

THAT sensuous profile was mocking her, coming closer and closer. Rowan felt panic rise and struggled to get away from the cruel smile, the icy eyes. She felt someone tugging, pulling her back, and suddenly found herself being jerked back to reality by a very definite and persistent pulling at her skirt.

Rowan opened her eyes. They felt gritty and tired. She was on the plane. She must have fallen asleep. The tugging registered again. She looked down, straight into the huge violet-coloured eyes of her son. Her heart stopped. And started again painfully. He was trailing an old and faded blanket. His cheeks were still sleep-flushed, his hair standing up. And her heart clenched so tight for a second that she felt in serious danger of fainting again. She willed it down.

Hungrily her eyes roved over him, as if checking a newborn for all his fingers and toes. She longed to pull him up and hold him close but didn't. She knew it might scare him. Just this moment alone was worth everything—put things into perspective. Isandro and his threats faded into the background.

Her voice was husky with emotion. 'Hi, Zac.'

One chubby hand clung to her leg for support. With his other hand he proudly mimicked her, pointing to himself. 'Zac!'

Then he put a hand to his head and made a face, obviously making the connection between Rowan and the previous day, when he'd fallen.

'That's right—you fell. Did you hurt your head?'

Zac nodded and rubbed his head. Rowan bent down and pretended to feel for a bump, exclaiming and making a fuss as if she'd found one. Her hands shook with the intensity of her emotions. Zac started to giggle.

Just then an older woman in a dark dress came up behind Zac. She looked Spanish. She bent down and took Zac's hand to lead him away, looking curiously at Rowan.

'I'm María—Zac's nanny…'

Rowan held out her hand. 'I'm Rowan…' She balked then. What did she say? *I'm Zac's mother? I'm Mrs Salazar?*

But the nanny didn't wait for elaboration. She smiled, shaking Rowan's hand perfunctorily. 'Excuse me—he needs to have something to eat.'

Rowan nodded jerkily and waved goodbye to Zac, who was already speeding off, his interest taken by something else. She turned back and looked sightlessly out of the window at the blanket of whiteness. She was too numb for tears and her heart ached. Yet she couldn't help but feel deep-seated relief at seeing Zac so well and healthy. That had always been her only priority…to see him flourishing so beautifully…it justified her decisions. Not that she'd ever needed justification. She'd acted from day one on a primal instinct that had been so strong she'd had no choice but to follow it. Above all she hadn't wanted him to suffer a moment's pain, which a selfishly prolonged departure would undoubtedly have brought. Even for a baby.

The one thing she hadn't counted on was *this*. Being in this situation. She wondered if she was being selfish coming back, seeking Zac out…wanting to get to know him. She knew rationally that she wasn't, but somehow she still didn't feel deserving of this. This luxury of seeing her son, this happiness. Perhaps she should have stayed away, said nothing. Let them get on with their lives. But with shameful weakness she knew she hadn't had the strength to do that. As soon as she had known that things were different, that she had a chance…

'You were hungry?'

Rowan's head whipped around. She'd been so caught up in her thoughts she hadn't heard Isandro come and sit down in the seat across the aisle. He was tieless and jacketless again, as if being in a suit even for a short time constrained his vibrant male energy. His shirt was open at the throat, revealing the strong brown column…. What was wrong with her? Although she'd been undeniably attracted to Isandro from the moment she'd first seen him, she couldn't remember experiencing this carnal level of attraction before.

'Yes. Starving.' She glanced at her plate, which was wiped clean of the delicious paella and salad she'd been served.

Isandro frowned as he recalled her curled up figure on the couch last night. There was something defenceless about the image that tugged at him. He ignored it. 'You didn't eat at the hotel?'

Rowan flushed and shook her head as his eyes ran up and down her form disparagingly.

'You've lost weight.'

He sounded accusing, and Rowan bristled. 'I know.'

He didn't have to spell out with that look just how unappealing she was to him. In that moment a blur of blond launched itself at Isandro, and deftly he plucked Zac up into his arms before he could do some damage or bump into something.

He glanced over to Rowan, showing the first tiny chink of something approximating warmth. 'As you've seen already, he's at the stage where he hasn't quite got the ability to stop once he's started.'

Rowan felt a lump come into her throat as she saw Zac wrap his arms around Isandro's neck, hugging him close only to just as abruptly squirm his way down Isandro's body, toddling off again under Isandro's watchful gaze until his nanny reclaimed him. The easy intimacy between them was a reminder of something she'd once foolishly allowed herself to believe in, and she could see now how potent it was when it was truly lavished on someone else. All she'd experienced however had been the surface emotion. Not the depth.

She couldn't quite meet his look. 'You've done an amazing job. He's beautiful.'

'Surprised?' came the dry response.

Rowan looked up, her eyes snared by his. She shook her head. 'No. I had no doubt that you would be a good father—' She stopped herself abruptly because she'd been about to say *My only concern was that you would not make enough time for him...* But that would have been revealing too much, and she could lay that fear to rest now. Clearly Isandro thought nothing of taking Zac with him on business trips.

Something in her tone made Isandro's eyes narrow on her for a second. Her eyes seemed to swirl with something indefinable, and for the first time since seeing her again he saw shadows, depths that hadn't been there before. *Pain?*

She looked away for a moment, and when she looked back her eyes were clear. They were so like Zac's that it took his breath away momentarily. But the ambiguity in their depths had gone. A trick of the light. That's all it had been.

At that point the hostess came to tell them the plane was preparing to land. When she had moved away, Isandro surprised Rowan by moving swiftly out of his seat to crouch in front of hers, a hand on either arm of her seat, effectively trapping her.

She could feel the heat from his body. Instinctively she pulled back into the seat, feeling claustrophobic. He was looking up at her with such intensity that she had to force herself to speak— 'What? What is it…?'—just to try and veer her mind off the dangerous track of previous experiences…moments when he'd looked at her before with that same intensity.

His eyes held her with all the easy hypnotism of a magician. His voice was deceptively light. His words were anything but.

'Just this, Rowan. If you come close to doing *one thing* to endanger, hurt or harm a hair on Zac's head then, believe me, not a court in this world will grant you custody when we divorce. I won't hesitate to use the full force of my power, and you'll be lucky if you even get to read about him in the papers as he grows up.'

He smiled, and it was so cold that Rowan could only stare. Transfixed by this absolute stranger. Then he stood and moved to a seat at the back of the plane with the effortless grace of a panther. Rowan stared at the place where he'd been. She felt cold inside. What would Isandro say if he knew she'd already laid down her life in order to protect Zac? Not much, she guessed bleakly. As he'd said himself, nothing would ever absolve her of that crime in his eyes. Rowan sighed and looked out of the window, just as the plane landed with a bump on Spanish soil.

Their journey to the east of Seville did not take long. Rowan looked out on the rolling plains of La Campina, barely able to take in the surroundings, still struggling to absorb everything that was happening. Isandro drove the Jeep. She was in the front, and María was in the back with Zac in his car seat. The bodyguard, who had been introduced to Rowan as Hernán, followed behind in another vehicle.

She was momentarily diverted when they entered the exquisitely picturesque town of Osuna, Isandro's birthplace and home.

'It's beautiful.'

'Yes.' Isandro glanced at her briefly but she didn't notice, too enthralled with the tiny, winding, climbing streets. He'd been watching her surreptitiously as they'd driven out of Seville, waiting for her reaction of dismay at leaving civilisation behind, but she hadn't given anything away. If anything she'd seemed uncomfortable with the bustling crowds— jumpy…almost slightly overwhelmed. But then he hadn't expected her to be so obvious so early.

They were at the top of the town now, overlooking the impressive baroque-style municipal buildings. Isandro took a quiet road which Rowan soon realised was a cul-de-sac. They came to a set of wrought-iron gates, with high walls on either side, overhung with trees. Isandro entered a code into a security pad from the window of the Jeep, the gates swung open and a security guard came out of a hut to greet Isandro, who waved back.

Rowan was not prepared for what appeared around the bend. She'd vaguely expected some kind of *hacienda*. Instead she saw a huge baroque mansion, emerging like something from a medieval fantasy. Cream-coloured, it seemed to shimmer in the sunlight, windows glinting, a profusion of flowers tumbling from pots along the steps and front of the house. Her jaw dropped. Isandro had parked and was already out of the Jeep, walking around the front to get Zac out of his seat in the back. Zac was bouncing up and down with excitement, having been cooped up for too long and clearly recognising home.

Rowan got out slowly, and the huge front door opened as if by magic, to reveal waiting staff. With trepidation in her breast she followed her husband and son into the house.

After a quick succession of introductions that had left Rowan's head spinning slightly, Isandro issued a stream of instructions and Rowan found herself being ushered upstairs, the housekeeper following with her bag. Rowan tried to take it from her, but she was having none of it. The chattering of Zac faded behind her as she was shown into her room.

It was a haven of dusky cream and rose. For some reason that she couldn't quite put her finger on at that moment the colours soothed her. And then it hit her. It wasn't the dreaded white of her nightmares. Of her recent past.

The housekeeper was showing her where everything was, and she welcomed the distraction from her inner demons. After she'd left, Rowan took a deep, steadying breath and explored for herself. A huge antique four-poster double bed had white muslin drapes caught back with ornate ties. The room had typically floral baroque features which were toned down by the simple colours. She went to the open French doors and took in the sight laid out before her with wide eyes, walking out as if in a trance.

A small stone balcony with ancient steps led down to a private inner courtyard, complete with a small pool inlaid with dark green tiles and glittering mosaics. She moved down the steps slowly, in awe of the stillness and beauty. The pool was surrounded by flowering bushes and olive trees. Scent hung heavy on the air. It was like something out of a dream she'd always had but never realised until now. Turning around in a circle, taking it in, she started when she saw Isandro standing with hands in his pockets outside another set of double doors, just feet from her own, with an identical balcony and steps leading down into the courtyard. His room? Her heart seized at that thought.

He came towards her, every step resonating with barely leashed menace. Rowan couldn't step back or she'd end up in the pool.

'You like what you see?' he asked tightly.

Rowan nodded, barely aware of what he was asking, her mouth suddenly dry at seeing him against this backdrop. He looked *golden*. Vibrant.

'You really messed up, you know.' He took one hand out of his pocket and gestured around them abruptly. 'You could have had all this the last two years, and now it will never be yours.'

Rowan's heart twisted in her chest. He thought she wanted this—the material evidence of his wealth. She started to shake her head, but couldn't get a word out. The sneer on his face stopped her.

'Just don't forget, dearest wife, that you are here purely at my behest and on the advice of my lawyers. They think it will serve me well to show how magnanimous I'm being in allowing you to get to know Zac, despite what you did. So don't get greedy and imagine for a second that you are entitled to a square inch of this place. You will not make a move that isn't watched and controlled. You will see Zac when and only when I allow it.'

Rowan forced her mouth to work, wanting to stop his words. 'That's all I want. I'm not here to take anything from you, Isandro. I don't have any interest in anything you own. My interest lies purely in Zac.'

He made a small rude sound. 'And in what you can make from the spoils of a divorce. Give me a break, Rowan. If I'd been less blinkered, less taken in by your innocent act of naivety, I would have realised long ago—'

'You'd have realised what?' she interjected bitterly, her emotions bubbling up, 'That the woman you married purely to raise your own standing in English society was just that— nothing but a trophy wife?' She'd known her actions when leaving would paint her in the worst possible light, and she knew she was being irrational, but the fact that he so easily believed her to be that kind of person lacerated her insides.

Isandro was momentarily taken aback. Her words brought back all his own humiliation—and he hated to admit it— his *disappointment*. And yet as she stood here now in front of him, a faint line of perspiration along her upper lip, her arms crossed defensively, pushing her breasts up, all he could think of was the desire pooling low in his abdomen. As much as he wanted to reject her in every way possible, he knew that with each moment spent together desire was growing stronger…

The disturbing arrow of lust he felt firmed his resolve. If he had but known it, he would have realised that the hot passion lying in wait beneath her cool exterior was a sign of things to come. She might have been a virgin on their wedding night, but he'd awoken her, and as soon as she'd been free of her baby she'd run. He'd never planned on their marriage being consummated, but when it had it had felt so right. And then when she'd become pregnant— He cut off his runaway thoughts and let hard ruthlessness rise. This woman in front of him represented his one fatal weakness.

'Our marriage was never meant to be anything but a business arrangement. You knew that. I knew that.'

'Of course it wasn't. I did know that…' Rowan gulped miserably, unable to continue for a moment, furious with herself for allowing him to goad her. The last thing she wanted was to draw his attention to her vulnerability to him. Or to the memory of how wanton she'd been during their short-lived marriage. Or to hear him say it had been a mistake. 'I never expected anything more.'

She felt hot in the afternoon sun as it beat down on her head. Hot and tired. She didn't have the energy for this. She didn't have to remind herself how clinical their conversations had been before the wedding. Didn't have to remind herself of how their marriage had never been meant to turn physical. *And yet it had.* She'd thrown herself at him. Shame clawed her insides.

In a series of meetings and dinners before they'd married Isandro had made everything crystal-clear. His words were still etched into her brain.

'I am marrying you so that I can save your father from bankruptcy, and by doing so I will take his position as CEO of Carmichael's Bank. You are marrying me in order to fulfil the terms of your mother's will and receive your maternal inheritance. As this won't be a real marriage, if I take a lover I will do so with the utmost discretion, and I would ask the same of you. In a year we can review things, talk about a divorce. A year with you by my side should be enough to establish my place. By then we will have both got what we wanted and my control of the bank will be assured.'

At the time Rowan had blinked at him slowly, finding it hard to move her gaze from his mouth to his eyes. Eyes which had been cool—cool enough to dampen her silly, girlish ardour. She'd been sitting there daydreaming, imagining him saying…*what*? That he'd fallen in love with her the minute he'd seen her and known she was the one for him? That he was as overwhelmed with lust for her as she was for him?

She returned to the present and swayed betrayingly as the heat seemed suddenly to intensify. Little had she known just how inconsequential she had been to him—that at no point had he *ever* entertained the possibility of feelings, no matter what she might have fooled herself into believing…

With an almost rough movement, Isandro took Rowan's arm and ushered her back up the crumbling steps and into her room. 'You need to get out of the sun. You're not used to the heat.'

She stood away from him, feeling better now that she was back inside, and looked at him warily.

He put distance between them, rocking back on his heels, tall and dominant. He laughed harshly. 'Silly me—how would I know what you're used to? After all, you could have been anywhere for the last two years.'

Rowan blanched. She knew she would have to tell him sooner or later exactly where she had been. But right now, feeling so rawly vulnerable, coming to terms with everything, was not the time. If she could just stay out of his way for the moment, focus on Zac... When she was feeling more in control of herself and her see-sawing emotions she would tell him then. Because when she did, it was going to invite all sorts of questions. Questions she certainly wasn't equipped emotionally to answer yet.

He backed away from her to a door she hadn't noticed in the wall as it was painted the same colour, almost camouflaged. It must be the adjoining door to his room. Her heart stopped and started again painfully. He saw her wide-eyed look. A smile mocked her.

'No one here expects us to pretend we're a happily married couple, enjoying the conjugal bed, so rest assured, Rowan. I won't be knocking on your door at night.'

No, she thought with an alarmingly sharp pain in the region of her heart. No doubt Isandro would have had a string of lovers to keep him company and must have a current one. She didn't have to remind herself of the disparaging remarks he had made about her to his sister. *That* conversation was a lane too far to travel down in her memory right now.

She breathed a sigh of relief when the door closed behind him, shutting away his disturbing presence. She sat on the bed, feeling exhausted, her mind a whirling minefield of memories. She pressed a hand to her chest, as if to slow down her thumping heart. To no avail. He had come to her room on their wedding night when she had least expected it. Had looked at her as if seeing her for the first time. She could still remember the aching longing she'd felt as his blue eyes had looked her up and down. She'd willed him to find her attractive, and she'd watched with bated breath as he'd come closer and closer. She'd known he'd come just to say goodnight, to be polite. But it had been as if her yearning body and heart had spoken out loud. And when, unbelievably, as if hearing her unspoken plea, he'd taken her in his arms…kissed her…he'd aroused a passion within her that still shocked and scared her to this day.

Rowan shook her head, as if she could somehow dislodge the painful images. She'd been so wanton, so full of ardour. With a groan Rowan stood jerkily and started to unpack, busying herself with the mundane task. It worked. Her feverish mind cooled. She gave in to the lure of a long hot shower, and afterwards belted a clean robe about herself and sank into the soft depths of the bed, letting the wave of blackness engulf her. She was with her son again. That was all that mattered. It had to be, because she couldn't hope for anything more.

She was back in that room. The white room. Two sets of double doors. She knew she had to get out, that if she didn't get out she'd never leave, never see her baby again. Panic gripped her, making her movements clumsy. She couldn't seem to get off the bed. She could hear footsteps approach, and knew they were coming to lock her in. Two sets of doors. She tried to scream, but no sound emerged. Her voice was gone. The covers on the bed were hampering her, trapping her. With the scream strangled in her throat Rowan felt salty hot tears fall down her face, and then she was being shaken. Terror froze her limbs…

Rowan became conscious of two things at once. It was the dream. The same dream, although a slightly different version.

It was just the dream. And she *was* being shaken. Her eyes flew open and clashed immediately with glacial blue ones. Isandro looked down at her, impatience stamped all over his face. She was in Spain, not in that awful room.

'What the hell is wrong with you? You were almost screaming the house down. Zac is asleep just across the hall.'

Zac.

The terror of the dream was still so real that she shuddered. She felt completely disorientated. It was dark—the curtains leading outside fluttered gently in the warm breeze. Isandro's big hands were still on her shoulders, his body half sitting on the bed, uncomfortably close enough for her to smell his scent, feel his heat. She jerked back.

'What time is it?'

He let her go when she moved, and glanced at the platinum watch encircling one wrist.

'Half past eleven.'

Rowan shook her head. 'At *night*?'

He nodded and stood up. 'Julia, the housekeeper, looked in on you at dinnertime, but you were sound asleep so I told her to leave you alone.' He studied her, and then asked harshly, 'What is it? Are you jetlagged?'

Rowan shook her head. 'No. Just…tired. It was just a bad dream. I…I had no idea I was crying out.' She put a hand to her temple. It was throbbing slightly. She became aware she was dressed in nothing but the robe and it was gaping open. She pulled it closed and awkwardly got up off the bed. 'I must have been more tired than I realised, that's all.'

Isandro put on the small bedside light and it threw long shadows across the room and his autocratic face. Rowan could see that he was still in his clothes.

'I was on my way to bed when I heard you.'

'Oh…' She felt as if he'd read her mind, and a blush came up to stain her cheeks. 'I'm sorry.'

'If it's likely to happen again I'll have to move you to the other side of the house, away from Zac. If he gets woken at night he's impossible to put back down.'

'It won't.' Rowan sent up a silent prayer. The dreams were a regular occurrence. Mainly they were tinged with sadness, and she woke crying, but this one had been more intense. It must be just because of the recent events. 'Really,' she assured Isandro, wanting his disturbing presence to be gone. 'It won't happen again.'

Isandro looked at her. Her skin was pink, her hair sexily tousled. Had this been some sort of ruse? To lead him in here, to try and seduce him? Was she aware of her effect on him? Had she become practised in the art of seduction these last two years? That thought made something knot deep in his gut. He couldn't put out of his mind the way she had felt under his hands just now, the frailty of her bones. Her clean, slightly musky scent. And yet the terror in her voice had been real enough, and the sound of her screams.

'See that it doesn't.' His voice sounded constricted to his own ears, and he was aware of the irrationality of his statement. If she had been in the grip of a genuine nightmare, of course she wouldn't be able to control her responses. He turned and left the room, shutting the door behind him. Damn the woman for coming back.

Isandro went across the hall and pushed open Zac's door, looking in to see his son sleeping peacefully, half on the bed, half off. He went over and placed him back safely in the middle, his heart swelling with love for this little boy. He hated the fact that he had to dance to Rowan's tune—hated the fact that as Zac's mother she could be allowed access to a child she had so callously walked away from. His hands clenched into fists. He had no choice but to allow her this access, but God help her if she thought he was going to allow her to take him away.

The following morning Rowan felt groggy, her head heavy. She had woken to a knock on the door, and now looked as a young maid came into the room. She pulled back the drapes farther, letting sunlight stream into the room, and opened the French doors wider. A bird called outside. Warmth came in on the light breeze and Rowan felt herself respond to it instinctively, letting it into her bones. It felt *good*.

'*Buenos Días.*'

'*Buenos Días.*' Rowan echoed, sitting up in the bed. She smiled at the girl hesitantly, and was rewarded with a shy smile. She was informed that breakfast would be served downstairs in fifteen minutes.

After a quick shower, and dressing in a plain skirt and T-shirt—one of about three outfits she owned—Rowan went downstairs. She felt self-conscious, well aware that she must look shabby. She just hadn't had to worry about clothes in so long, and she certainly hadn't expected to be *here*. Her mind flew from those concerns as she approached what must be the dining room door. She could hear the shouts of Zac.

With her heart thumping painfully she took a deep breath and went in. Two sets of eyes turned towards her. One she did her best to block out and one a mirror image of her own. She focused on Zac as she came in, unable to help a smile from spreading across her face. He was a mess, with food everywhere—all over him and his face. He grinned up at her from his high chair as she approached the table.

For one very normal and wry moment she didn't doubt for a second that his winning grin could change in an instant to tears and tantrums. But even that thought made her heart twist, and the longing to just sit and study every single aspect of him was overwhelming with its force.

Reluctantly she looked away and greeted María, who sat on the other side of the table, also eating breakfast. The woman sent her a hesitant smile, and Rowan reciprocated, feeling grateful. She sat down, and the housekeeper bustled in with a plate heaped high with food. She indicated to where there was fruit, croissants, and poured Rowan some steaming and fragrant coffee.

'I trust you slept well?'

Rowan glanced briefly at Isandro, whose tone was as arctic as his eyes. 'Yes, thank you. The room is more than comfortable.'

María broke the uncomfortable ensuing silence. 'It is a stunning house. I've often thought it must have been a magical place to grow up. Zac is very fortunate.'

Isandro slid a mocking glance at Rowan, and then a more benign one to María. 'Yes, isn't he?'

Rowan felt the weight of a myriad insults in that comment, but either María was oblivious to the tension or else she was a very good actress, and she chattered on about the house, asking questions. In truth Rowan was relieved that the other woman was there, to divert Isandro's attention from her.

Isandro was deftly feeding Zac, making all sorts of emotions run through Rowan. In answer to something María said which Rowan hadn't heard, he said, 'This isn't my original family home. My sister lives there, on the other side of Osuna, with her family and my mother.'

Rowan's insides clenched in instinctive self-protection at the mention of his mother and sister. At least they didn't live *here*. Relief flooded her. She needed to be thankful for small mercies. As it was she was sure she'd have to face them sooner or later, and she didn't believe that time and circumstance would have made either of them any more amenable to her.

Just then María stood up, excusing herself. Isandro stood too, and took Zac out of his high chair, handing him over. 'I think he's had all he's going to eat for now.'

'I'll take him up to get dressed…' The older woman deftly lifted him and took him out.

When Isandro sat down again Rowan's breath caught in her throat. She'd only just noticed that he was dressed down, in jeans and a T-shirt, the material doing little to disguise the breadth and power of his chest. He looked at her over the rim of his coffee cup.

'No more dreams last night?'

She shook her head. 'No.'

She looked away and down, and Isandro noticed the faint purple shadows under her eyes. Something kicked him in the chest as he recalled his impatience the previous night, and he did not welcome it.

'I'm sure,' he drawled conversationally, 'that it's just your guilty conscience.'

Rowan's head jerked up. His words had cut right through her with the precision of a knife.

For a second Isandro couldn't believe what he was seeing—abject pain in the depths of those deep violet eyes. He couldn't believe it because it wasn't there, he told himself. Wasn't he already witnessing her shy, hesitant smiles with Zac? The way she was charming María…?

'Isandro…' Rowan's voice felt unused and too husky. 'All I ask is for a chance. That's all. I'm here on your terms. I won't do anything you don't want me to do. I just want a chance. That's all.'

He sat back in his chair and saw her ramrod-straight back, her tightly held body. It was too thin. The shortness of her hair highlighted her long neck, and the bones in her wrist seemed so fragile—as if he might break them just by taking hold…

'You're getting the best chance you'll ever get or deserve. You're here, aren't you?' he gritted out. He hated being so aware of her.

She nodded and looked down, her hair falling forward across one cheek to shield her eyes from him. He had to stop himself from putting out a hand to pull it back, tuck it behind her ear.

'Thank you.'

He had to get out of there, away from her sham act of vulnerability. Abruptly Isandro stood from the table, dropping his napkin. He looked at Rowan sternly. 'You're here, as I said, primarily because I have no choice—and also because I know you won't last a week.' His eyes flicked disparagingly over her worn clothes. 'All this effort and play-acting…you really don't need to bother, you know.'

He turned, about to walk out of the door, and Rowan gathered her strength from somewhere, storing her hurt at his words deep down. She stood up, the sound of the chair harsh on the floor.

'Wait.'

He stopped and turned, impatience and intransigence stamped on every line of his body.

'When…when can I spend time with Zac, please?'

She held her breath. If he was going to refuse her—

'You can see him for a couple of hours before he goes down for his afternoon nap.'

He walked back in then, and came to stand close. Rowan gripped the table with one hand, slightly off balance after the way she had stood up.

'I'm off work for one week, Rowan. I'll be around, watching your every move, so don't get any ideas.'

Rowan watched as he walked away again, and out of the room. *Off work for one week?* Since when had he taken more than a day off work? She sat down again, trembling all over.

Had having Zac been what it took to make him change? Because undoubtedly he had. It was that softness she'd noticed. Not directed at her, by a long shot, but a softness nevertheless, and certainly a different attitude to work if this behaviour was anything to go by.

But she had seen it before, and it was this side of him, so rarely on display, which had given her the confidence to leave Zac—because she'd known above all else that he wanted and would love his son. The first time she'd really seen that side of him had been with his sister's children, who must be aged three and five now. He'd had an innate patience and an ability to communicate with them that had surprised Rowan when she'd seen them together at the wedding. It had bowled her over. And after she'd conceived, on their wedding night, she'd known instinctively that he'd be a good father.

Despite the fact that he'd been so ambitious that he had coldly married her in order to take control of one of the biggest banks in England, he'd welcomed the news of impending fatherhood. Clearly, though it had never been expected from her, he'd been happy to be having an heir.

She'd been halfway in love with him before they'd even married, and that had coloured her own decision to allow herself to be persuaded into the cold business deal of a marriage. Not that she'd had much choice... But when it had turned physical, and she'd fallen pregnant, then she'd foolishly and naively hoped for so much more.

She angrily took a sip of her tepid coffee, not wanting to remember but unable to forget. Her ailing father had pointed him out to her at that function in London's Savoy Hotel. But in truth she'd seen him the minute he'd come into the room. Anyone there with a pulse had. He'd appeared like a golden lion in the midst of lesser beings, mortals. There had been a moment's hush before the energy and conversation had zinged up a few notches. All the women had gone into preen mode; all the men had paled into insignificance. And he had just stood there, eyes constantly roving, assessing, blatantly uninterested in the conversation around him. Faintly sneering.

Rowan had been unable to take her eyes off him. Like every other woman there, she didn't have to remind herself. And yet she'd caught his eye—*or so she had stupidly thought*—and he had walked over towards her with singular intent. Rowan had been shaking, trembling, her eyes huge when he'd stopped in front of her and she'd finally realised that he wasn't looking at her, he'd been looking at her father. With the briefest of acknowledgements for Rowan—and she could remember the way those cool eyes had flicked over her—he and her father had shaken hands and retired to a private room, where they had hashed out the deal. The deal that had included her and changed her life.

She could still remember her misery when she'd over-heard some women talking in the powder room shortly after-wards. 'Did you see Rowan Carmichael's face when he walked over? The girl practically had her tongue hanging out. I mean, really, who would have her? She's twenty-five and still a virgin, I bet! And that dress—*honestly*. I wouldn't be surprised if it had been her mother's…'

They had gone on and on for what seemed like ages. When Rowan had emerged she'd gone straight outside and taken a cab home, her confidence in ribbons.

Rowan realised that she was gripping the small coffee cup so tight that she was in danger of breaking it. She relaxed her hold and put it down, took in a deep breath. So much had happened since then. *So much.* She couldn't allow being here to bring back those memories. She had to focus on the present and *Zac*. That was how she would get through this.

CHAPTER FOUR

'FORGIVE me, Mrs Salazar, it's just that…this situation is a little unusual.'

Rowan grimaced inwardly at the way María had immediately called her Mrs Salazar in her broken English. She tried out her rusty Spanish. 'Please, María—call me Rowan.' She looked at the other woman with sympathy. 'I know it must be strange for you to suddenly have me arrive like this, but my only concern is Zac and getting to know him.'

The other woman was obviously taken aback to hear Rowan speak Spanish, but still looked tense, worried. Not sure how to handle this situation.

'Look,' said Rowan, 'all I want to do is spend time with you and Zac for the moment. After all, he doesn't know me, so he's going to have to get used to me.'

A look of relief crossed María's face, and she wondered if Isandro had told her not to let Zac out of her sight while Rowan was there? She wouldn't put it past him.

María started to tell her what their routine was as Zac happily played on the lawn with an array of toys, mainly cars. Rowan could feel the back of her neck prickle, but didn't turn around. She was very aware that Isandro would be watching from one of the windows that looked out onto the main lawn.

She firmly pushed all thoughts of her husband out of her head. She had two hours with Zac today, and she was going to make the most of it. She also pushed down the well of emotion that threatened to erupt on a continuous basis every time she looked at her beautiful sturdy son. His personality was already ingrained, strongly apparent. More than a hint of his father. He toddled over to her and she shot a reassuring smile to María as she let him take her by the hand so he could pull her down onto the ground to help him play with his cars.

Isandro looked out of the window, arms folded tightly across his chest. He watched as Zac appeared to be happily welcoming Rowan into his life—as if she hadn't walked away from him, as if she hadn't already *rejected* him in his most vulnerable moment.

Rage burned upwards on behalf of his son, and he had to restrain himself from going out there and pulling Zac away from her grasping hands. And yet…he looked happy. And she wasn't looking bored or irritated. He hated to admit it, but Zac was naturally cautious with strangers and yet with Rowan, from that first moment in the hotel, he'd shown none of that caution—almost as if he'd recognised her. Isandro shook his head. That couldn't be possible…

Rowan was down on the ground, patiently nodding as Zac babbled incoherently with all the seriousness of a child on a mission who believed himself to be absolutely understood. She was still dressed in that tatty skirt and T-shirt, and the skirt was riding upwards to show a long length of leg, pale and smooth. His insides contracted, and resolve hardened inside him. He turned abruptly from the window and strode to his desk to pick up the phone.

The following day Rowan went back into the house. Zac had just been taken away for his nap. She hurried through the hall, thinking that maybe one day she would be able to spend time with Zac and not feel as though her heart were being ripped from her chest every time she looked at him.

Her foot was on the bottom step of the main stairs when she heard her name being called autocratically. There was to be no respite, then. It was as if Isandro was some sort of magician, catching her at her most vulnerable moments. She turned reluctantly and hoped her eyes didn't look too bright. Isandro stood framed in what she guessed to be his study door—she could see a big desk in the background.

'Could you come in here, please?' His tone made a mockery of the *please*.

She nodded briefly, tersely, and walked towards him, avoiding his eyes. He stood back to let her pass and she held her breath, not wanting to breathe in his scent. His essence. For a second she was so wrapped up in trying to avoid being aware of him that she didn't even see the man who had stood and was now holding out a hand. Isandro was introducing him.

'This is my lawyer, Ricardo Sanchez.'

Rowan stepped forward to shake his hand, still a little stunned that she hadn't even noticed him. 'Señor Sanchez.'

Her heart stopped and started again. The divorce papers. It had to be. She felt a self-protecting numbness spread through her. Even though she'd been expecting this from the moment they'd come to Spain, still it shocked her that he was giving her no time to prove herself…that he was carrying out his threat.

'Please sit down, Rowan.'

Rowan sat heavily into the seat that had been brusquely indicated by Isandro, and watched as he walked around the desk and sat down. Even in jeans and a T-shirt he looked formidable, frighteningly powerful. The sun slanted in at that moment and gilded his hair with a dark golden aura. She blinked and looked away to his lawyer, who was seated to her right. He was relatively young—she guessed him in his mid-forties—and handsome, albeit in a very buttoned-up way. He looked at her then, and smiled. Rowan was momentarily taken aback at this common courtesy after the past forty-eight hours of tension, and she smiled back, her mouth feeling strange in the movement.

'Ricardo.'

The name was called in a staccato of impatience. Rowan flushed and looked away, feeling guilty and not knowing why.

Isandro glared at her, and then at his lawyer. 'If you wouldn't mind showing my wife the papers, please?'

'Of course.' Isandro's lawyer bent and smoothly pulled out a sheaf of papers. He handed one set to Isandro, another to Rowan, and kept one himself.

They were in Spanish, but Rowan could make out the unmistakable. They were indeed the divorce papers. Something hard and unyielding settled into her chest, making her feel slightly breathless.

'I think you will find that everything is in order. Very standard.' Bitterness tinged Isandro's voice. 'Your entitlement under the prenup is unchanged. After careful consideration I fear that it will only cause more trouble than it's worth to fight your right to it—which undoubtedly I could do after your…disappearing act.'

Rowan looked up, her hands clenching around the papers. 'Isandro, I've already told you that—'

He flicked a lean hand, cutting her off with the violence of his gesture. 'Spare us. Señor Sanchez is well aware of the circumstances. Your acting isn't necessary here.'

She glanced to the other man, who now avoided her eye

and looked uncomfortable. Very well. Isandro wasn't going to listen to her. If he insisted on giving her the money then she would simply lodge it straight into a trust account for Zac, and perhaps give some to—

'So, if you could just sign the back page here…'

Rowan looked at Isandro incredulously, to see that he had flipped back the numerous pages filled with technical legalese to point to a dotted line. Indignation coursed through her. 'You have got to be kidding me.'

Isandro slammed down the papers, brows drawn together. 'If you're thinking of turning on an act to try and make me believe that you don't want this—'

Rowan stood up jerkily, every cell screaming at her not to let him see how this was affecting her. How hard it was for her to be faced with the stark reality of their marriage ending for ever. 'Of course I'm not. But do you really think I am so stupid that I would meekly allow you to shove this under my nose and expect me to sign it without so much as a by-your-leave?' She threw the papers down on the table as if they'd stung her, terrified that he'd see them shaking in her hands. 'It's entirely in Spanish, which isn't my first language—'

'You're fluent—'

'Yes, I am—but not in legal terms. How do I know you haven't added in a clever clause about custody, signing away my rights to Zac?'

He stood now too, and bristled at her from across the desk. Clearly she'd piqued his honour.

'Of course I haven't. These are divorce papers, pure and simple.'

'Well, I'm not signing a single thing until I've spoken to my own solicitor and he's looked them over. When he says they're okay, then I'll sign.'

Isandro felt impotent. Caught. And yet he knew that what

she said made sense. In another circumstance, if she were a different person, he would have advised her to take exactly the course of action she'd just outlined.

In Spanish, Rowan heard the lawyer say nervously, 'She's right. We need to send a copy to her own people.'

Rowan looked down at Isandro's lawyer. 'And you can send them in English. I won't take on the added expense of my solicitor having to bring in a translator.' Her bravado was masking intense pain.

'Of course,' the other man assured her, with something approaching respect in his dark eyes.

She looked back to Isandro. 'I'd also like to ring Mr Fairclough now, to advise him of this.'

She'd hitched up her chin, and with her arms crossed defensively Isandro felt inexplicably as if he should apologise. He quashed it down. This woman had committed a crime that not many would forgive. What right had she to be coming over all moral with him? He clenched his jaw and picked up the phone, handing her the receiver. She just looked at it. And then back to him.

'*In private.*' Her tone could have peeled paint from the walls.

Isandro looked at her for a long moment. The tension tautened and crackled. Rowan felt a little sorry for Señor Sanchez.

It didn't sit well with Isandro at all that he'd acted so out of character. But he couldn't deny the visceral way she made him feel. It had led him to convene this meeting, to get papers drawn up in record time. He spoke with exaggerated courtesy. 'I'll have one of the maids bring a cordless phone to your room. You will have all the privacy you need there.'

'Thank you.'

And with her head held high Rowan stalked out of the room. She sagged once outside, though, and then hurried up the stairs, almost as if Isandro might call her back, or bring her back bodily and force her to sign. She knew that no matter what had happened he wouldn't have done something so underhand as to add in a clause regarding custody. It wasn't his style. And yet she knew she was right to assert herself. She'd be a fool if she let him think he could walk all over her.

Once in her room, she went and stood by the open doors and looked out onto the courtyard. Its beauty and hushed stillness soothed her. And made her aware of the pain in her heart. The pain that had lodged there when it had become so blatantly obvious that Isandro would have divorced her there and then if he'd had the choice. Got rid of her as if she was nothing more than a piece of gum under his shoe. She shouldn't even be feeling like this. If she was, then it meant that—

A brief knock came at the door, startling her, and she opened it to reveal the maid who had woken her the other morning. She took the cordless phone with a strained smile, dug out David Fairclough's number and made the call. She explained briefly what had happened, and warned him to expect to receive divorce papers.

That done, she took a deep, shuddering breath. This was it. The beginning of the end. The beginning of the end of their marriage of convenience. Of a marriage that had never been meant to be consummated, that should never have resulted in a baby. But it had. And she didn't regret that for a second. Not even when it had caused her more pain and grief than she'd believed herself capable of enduring. And she would keep enduring it until she had proved herself to Isandro and come to some arrangement whereby she could live her own life *and* see Zac—be a part of his life too.

For the rest of that week Rowan avoided Isandro as much as possible. She saw him at breakfast, and in the evenings, when they would conduct stilted conversations at dinner. But for the rest of the time he would either be shut up in his office, out riding, or with Zac.

She relished her short time with Zac every day, when she got to see him before his nap. And relished even more how María was obviously feeling more relaxed with her presence, more inclined to use the time that Rowan had with Zac as a little break for herself. She'd bring a book and read as Zac and Rowan played.

Today, though, as María was taking Zac away for his nap, he let out a cry of distress, clearly wanting to keep playing with Rowan. Her heart broke. María smiled sympathetically. 'He's taken to you in a big way. But I'm afraid Señor Salazar's instructions were explicit.'

'María, don't feel you have to explain. I'm here on your territory—and Zac's.'

The woman blushed uncomfortably as Zac still wailed in her arms. 'I know, but you seem…' She blushed again. '*Nice*. And you are his—'

'What's going on here?'

Their heads turned in unison, to see Isandro striding across the lawn. He took Zac from María and inspected his tear-stained face. The quivering lip.

María rushed to speak. 'He's just tired, Señor Salazar. It's time for his nap, but he was having too much fun playing with Row—' She stopped. '*Mrs* Salazar.'

Isandro looked from her to Rowan, as if he suspected something had happened. He looked so grimly protective that Rowan's heart lurched.

'I'll…I'll go inside. I don't want to upset him. María's right. He's just over-tired.'

Before he could say another word Rowan hurried inside. Feeling agitated and restless, she balked at going up to her room, where she always retreated every day. Instead she went into the main drawing room. She whirled around a moment later when she heard heavy footsteps and saw Isandro darkening the door, coming in to shut it behind him.

He advanced with lethal slowness, and Rowan backed away instinctively.

'What is it?' she asked flatly, because she had no doubt that Isandro was about to fill her in on her latest crime.

'What are you doing to my son?'

Rowan shook her head and it felt fuzzy. 'Nothing. Just playing with him.'

'He was upset. *You* must have upset him.'

Rowan's eyes grew round. She couldn't believe the unfairness of his attack. 'He was tired, that was all, Isandro. Children his age get over-excited easily. He's had someone new to play with this week. By next week the novelty will have worn off.'

Isandro scowled. Her reference to *next week* made all sorts of hackles rise. 'Since when did *you* know so much about kids?' His voice was scathing.

Rowan steeled herself to withstand it. 'I'm a woman. I've *au paired*. And apart from anything else he's my son. I—'

She stopped. She'd been about to say *I love him*, but knew that would bring down a whole torrent of abuse on her head.

'He's my son, Isandro,' she said simply instead. 'And you're going to have to get used to it. I'm not going anywhere. I'm going to be around for the rest of his life.'

Isandro raked his blistering blue gaze up and down. 'Until you've got your hands on what you came back for, you mean. Then he'll be dropped like a hot potato again, and this time it'll be worse because he'll have got to know you.' He swung away from her with a violent movement. 'I can't believe I'm allowing this—' He stopped, his voice full of self-recrimination, and came back close again, eyes blazing.

Rowan couldn't back away any more as a chair was behind her. He'd come so close that she could see the flecks of lighter blue in his eyes. Smell him. *Dear God.* If he knew for a second—

'I know what you're doing. But know this. With me as his protector you can be damn sure that if you so much as cause one tear of distress to fall from his eyes *you're gone.*'

Rowan's throat closed over as she felt a well of sadness rise up. She could feel Isandro's pain. His uncertainty. She could feel it because she'd been through it, a million times over. It was one of the reasons she'd walked away. She wanted to reach out and reassure him, and her hand even stretched out impulsively.

Immediately he jerked back. He looked at her hand suspended in the air as if it were toxic. Couldn't believe that he'd almost, for one second, responded to her gesture. 'Don't come near me. You disgust me.'

With a chilling look he turned and walked from the room.

Rowan couldn't move. She was locked in stasis. Paralysed by the venom in his expression just now. The very real evidence of his absolute hatred and unforgiveness. Hot tears filled her eyes, splashing down her cheeks. She pulled her hand in and cradled it against her chest as if he had struck it. Because, worse than anything else that had just happened, there was another emotion that she had to acknowledge. And it shamed her beyond belief. It had been jealousy. Jealousy of her own son. Because Isandro loved him so completely, so utterly, that she knew he had the capacity to do what she had done. Lay down his life for his child. And the fact that she represented that level of a threat to him hurt her more than she could bear.

For the last couple of days of Isandro's week off he had watched Rowan even more closely. Instead of leaving her alone with Zac and María in the afternoons, as he had done before, he joined them. His reluctance to leave Rowan unsupervised with Zac was palpable. It had made something harden inside her. She would not let him scare her. She was stronger than that. He didn't know how strong she'd had to become. So she endured his company, his looks, his obvious distrust.

Even so, her nerves were stretched to breaking point by the time Sunday night came. They were in the dining room drinking coffee, having finished dinner. Rowan took another sip and closed her eyes to savour the aroma and taste as much as to block Isandro out.

When Julia came in to bid them goodnight, Rowan got up quickly, wanting to leave, to avoid being subjected to more of Isandro's scathing looks, ascerbic comments. But a hand snaked out of nowhere and caught her wrist, enveloping it in shocking heat. The physical contact threw her so much that she stumbled backwards. If not for Isandro standing to catch her shoulders she would have fallen.

She looked up with startled eyes. His hands were like a brand, burning through the threadbare material of her thin sweater. He seemed to be caught too. His eyes flared. Rowan stopped breathing as the air around them seemed suddenly charged with electricity. It couldn't be. He despised her. And yet…*this* was what she'd felt that night. The night of their wedding. And countless nights over the months of her pregnancy. Nights of passion…white-hot consummation. The memories of which had become her fantasies.

In an instant he'd moved even closer, and one hand came off her shoulder to tip her chin upwards. To better see her face. Her neck seemed to be made of elastic as her head fell back.

'I wonder…'

'You wonder what…' Rowan croaked out.

'What tricks you've learnt in the past two years. For no doubt you've been busy becoming more *experienced*.'

CHAPTER FIVE

ISANDRO'S words didn't make sense at first, and it was only when his mouth was dropping towards hers, his eyes closing, that she realised what he was doing. She felt her body sway towards him, helpless. The sensation of wanting this, wanting him to kiss her, was so overwhelming, so intense that she couldn't help it.

And when his mouth touched hers softly, and then harder, his lips firming over hers, she gave a little moan of acceptance. Her own mouth opened under his, seeking for closer intimacy. Seeking for his tongue to find hers, seeking for his arms to pull her close and let her feel the strength of his body against hers. She'd craved this for so long. For ever. And had thought she'd never experience it again. She'd stored up her memories of this like a miser with her gold, taking it out every now and then, allowing herself to revel in it…guiltily.

Despite the clarity he'd felt when he'd started this, the reluctant yet insistent desire to prove something to himself, now Isandro's arms itched to pull her pliant and yielding body even closer. To feel her breasts crushed against his chest. He could feel her soft mouth opening, hesitantly, as if she was unsure…and like a douche of cold water he pulled back, so suddenly and harshly that Rowan stumbled backwards. This time, however, he made no move to steady her. He'd told her just the other day that she disgusted him, and yet he'd just proved otherwise. He hated that she'd made him lose control. Hated to be faced with the evidence that he still wanted her. Badly. In spite of her actions.

Cruelly he wiped a hand across his mouth, as if to wipe the imprint of her lips away. 'You've perfected the art of the virginal act, I see. It might almost lead me to believe that perhaps you were more experienced than I remember. It's not unknown for a woman to become so practised in the art that she can make every man feel like it's the first time.'

Rowan gasped, and struggled to contain her wildly see-sawing emotions. She was hurt beyond belief at the way he'd wiped away her kiss. Yet her body still hummed, felt raw with desire. How could she have just let him do that to her when his motives couldn't be anything but transparently hurtful to her? Hadn't the way he'd looked at her the other day in the drawing room had *any* effect? The words he'd said?

'How dare you—?'

She made to get past him, but he caught her arm, swinging her back. His face was harsh, the shadows in the room making his hair look dark. His lips thinning. The evidence of his own monumental lack of judgment where she'd been concerned struck him anew.

'You married me for no better reason than to secure your inheritance. But you tricked me, Rowan. You went one step too far. In a bid to secure your future for ever you got pregnant as an added insurance. With no intention of ever being there for your child.'

Rowan's voice shook, and she could barely mask her hurt and pain. 'You have it so wrong it's not even funny, Isandro.' She wanted to say something—anything to cut him down, minimise the hurt—but she had no defence. Because she knew well that even once she'd been pregnant nothing had diminished her passion. If her only aim had been to get pregnant, then why would she have thrown herself at him so ardently night after night?

So she used the only arsenal she could think of to distract him from that glaring anomaly. 'You're forgetting the little choice I had in the matter. It was part of the deal, remember? To ensure your social acceptance and save my father's face I *had* to marry you.'

He looked her up and down, took in the rapid rise and fall of her breasts. Her words made something jar uncomfortably inside him. Made something inexplicably painful surge upwards.

Rowan finally ripped her arm free. Right at that moment she hated him with an intensity that shook her to the core—but if she was honest she knew it just masked a much scarier emotion. This was exactly what she was protecting herself from. The fear that he would guess for even a second how much he did affect her. And had affected her.

'Go to hell, Isandro.'

He recovered himself. 'Not without taking you with me.'

I've already been there... The words trembled on her lips but she bit them back.

'I'm not going anywhere, Isandro. So get used to it.' And with those parting words she walked on jelly legs out of the room and upstairs.

That night she had the dream again. She was trapped in the white room. Couldn't get out. But when she woke with wet cheeks and her heart thumping she was alone, and thankful that she hadn't caused a disturbance as the house was silent.

The next day, as Isandro sat in his office in Seville, he felt an almost overpowering urge to leave, get into his car and go home. She was there, in his house. Alone and unsupervised apart from María and his staff. He could see that María had been confused as to how to treat her. He saw how Rowan had been twisting the other woman around her finger. Was he mad to leave her there? He stood up and ran a hand through his hair.

A call came through. He picked up the phone and barked into it.

'Good morning to you too.'

'What is it, Ricardo? I'm busy.'

His lawyer wasn't stupid. He took the hint. 'I thought you'd like to know that your wife's solicitor has instructed us that the papers are good for her to sign. He's just rung her at the house to inform her of this.'

Isandro sat down into his chair. An immediate heaviness had entered his chest. Which was ridiculous. He should be elated.

'Fine. They're still in my study at home. If you can meet me there tonight we'll sign them.'

'Of course.'

Isandro let the phone drop.

On the other end his lawyer smiled wryly. He wondered what would have been the reaction if he'd said no, that actually he had a date tonight? He shook his head. Men as powerful as Isandro were never given excuses. So he picked up his phone again and called off the date with his girlfriend.

With Isandro's disturbing presence out of the house, Rowan felt herself relaxing somewhat for the first time in days. She knew María had been given strict instructions not to allow Rowan any more time with Zac than had been discussed, but the woman bent the rules a little. Rowan was so pathetically grateful, it was ridiculous. Without Isandro looking over her shoulder she could really get to know Zac. She knew well, though, that it was galling for him to know she was there.

Every evening when he came back he looked in on Zac, and at her suspiciously, as if she might have done something to him.

Rowan had signed the preliminary divorce papers a couple of evenings ago, and since then a heaviness had weighed her down inside. But she told herself it was only natural to feel pain at the thought that she and Isandro wouldn't be able to provide Zac with a stable family...

Dinner on Friday evening passed off without incident, and Rowan managed to escape without being detained. Up in her own room, she was too restless to sleep and took confidence in the fact that Isandro would no doubt be in his study, working. She went out into the patioed garden and tipped her head back to see the stars, drinking in the night.

Suddenly weary and feeling very vulnerable, she sank for a moment onto the bottom step and let her head fall back. The warm Andalucian air caressed her. She closed her eyes and breathed in deeply. Until a sound made her head jerk up. She stood hurriedly when she saw a dark shape peel itself from the wall. She knew well who it was. A stranger would have caused less panic.

'Isandro.' Thank goodness her voice was steady.

'Did you think it might be a burglar?' he asked lightly.

Rowan held onto the wall beside her as he walked down his steps with leonine grace.

She shook her head and smiled tightly, thinking of all the bodyguards. 'With the security system here?'

He came and stood in front of her. She was still on the bottom step, so she stood slightly taller than him, and in the dark star-filled night she had a sudden urge to put her hands around his face, lower her mouth to his to kiss him and feel him put his arms around her waist.

She shook inwardly with the effort it took to clear her mind of the image.

'Isandro, what do you want?'

She couldn't read his face. But his eyes were hard. He opened his mouth to speak and she braced herself for censure but just then a noise sounded from inside Isandro's room. Someone calling his name. And the panic in that voice was unmistakable. Immediately Rowan recognised it, and hairs rose on the back of her neck. Everything else was forgotten.

'María…' she breathed. Instinctively she followed Isandro's swift return to his room, where María stood wringing her hands, her face as white as snow. Rowan could see that she was in shock and panic, almost about to faint.

Isandro went and took her shoulders, but the woman was incoherent. Rowan tried to get her to calm down.

'María what is it? Just try to breathe and tell us.'

Rowan could sense Isandro's swift sideways look of annoyance that she had followed him.

The other woman finally managed to say, '*Zac*—it's Zac. He's having some kind of fit—I don't think he's breathing.'

Shock slammed into Rowan even as she registered Isandro reacting like lightning and thrusting María aside. No… *No!* her mind screamed. Not now. Not after everything.

On numb legs she followed Isandro into Zac's room. She could see that Isandro was dangerously close to panic as well. With an instinct she wasn't even aware she possessed, she pushed him aside to have a look. María had followed them, clearly verging on full-blown hysteria. Rowan somehow forced herself to remain calm and look at Zac properly.

As she did, she felt an intense burst of relief. He had stopped convulsing and was now rigid on the bed, his skin turning blue. He was unconscious, but breathing. She stepped in front of Isandro and knelt down by the bed, quickly turning Zac towards her and onto his side. Then she loosened his pyjama top. Felt his forehead. He was burning up.

She looked at María and issued a rapid instruction. María just stood there, in shock. Rowan snapped out her name, and it woke María from her trance. She ran into the bathroom. That seemed to wake Isandro too. Rowan felt his hands on her shoulders, as if to pull her back. His voice was hoarse with fear.

'What are you doing? You're going to hurt him.'

Rowan shook him off. 'He's going to be fine. He's having a febrile convulsion. Go and call an ambulance or a doctor.'

She looked up at Isandro, who hadn't moved. He looked so pale that she felt scared. '*Go*—call an ambulance. We have to get him to hospital. He'll be awake by the time you come back, I promise.'

Her urgency finally penetrated, and he left the room. Rowan had instructed María to get a glass of cool water and a baby paracetamol. By the time Isandro came back Zac was indeed coming round.

Rowan felt shaky with relief. She made sure to keep him in the recovery position and spoke to him softly. He was groggy and disorientated, a little grumpy, which she knew could be expected after a convulsion. When she deemed him to be sufficiently recovered enough to swallow, she gave him the paracetamol María had brought, and made him drink some water.

'What's that?' Isandro stepped forward, his hands clenched by his sides. Rowan read his mood in an instant. He hated being impotent—hated seeing the power that she had just displayed.

'It's baby paracetamol. To bring down his temperature.'

Just then they heard banging on the door downstairs, and Rowan breathed a sigh of relief. María ran out. Rowan focused on Zac, making sure she was keeping him cool and comfortable.

When the paramedics arrived she explained what had happened. Isandro had lifted the still sleepy Zac into his arms to bring him downstairs, and they met the doctor, who had also arrived. He quickly checked Zac over and confirmed him safe enough to move.

Rowan stood at the door and watched as they got into the ambulance. She felt weak and limp in the aftermath. At the last minute the doctor looked at her. 'Aren't you the child's mother?'

Rowan stood up straight. 'Well…yes—yes, I am. But—'

'Well, you must come with us. The child will want you too, and he's going to be disorientated enough.'

'But—'

The doctor was impatient. 'You must come to tell them what happened so they can determine if it is serious enough to keep him in.'

Rowan's eyes met Isandro's, where he sat in the ambulance cradling Zac. His features were tight and drawn. 'He's right, Rowan. Get in.'

So she did. They travelled to the small local hospital some ten minutes away, and Rowan didn't take her eyes off her son. He was recovering rapidly. Rapidly enough so that by the time they had arrived at the hospital he was looking around him with big eyes, although still groggy.

After Zac had been thoroughly examined the doctor deemed that he should stay in overnight, just to be safe. Isandro immediately declared that he was staying with Zac. Rowan said nothing, just walked with María out to the front of the hospital. She'd followed them, with Hernán. The woman was inconsolable.

'I'm so sorry. I just froze. I got such a shock when I saw him convulsing…I *knew* what it was, but I've never seen it before…'

Rowan put her arm around María's shoulder. 'María, don't worry. You did the best thing by coming to get Isandro.'

María looked at her with something like awe in her eyes. 'But *you* knew what to do. *You're* his mother.'

'María, you should go home. And take Rowan with you.'

Rowan looked at Isandro. He had followed them out and he looked exhausted. She wouldn't fight with him now, but she had no intention of going home. Isandro went back inside, and she saw María out to the Jeep and sent her off. Then she went back inside too. She didn't go into Zac's room, where she guessed Isandro was, she just sat on a chair in the corridor. A different bodyguard hovered discreetly nearby. All she wanted was to be close, in case anything happened.

That was when she started to tremble. Uncontrollably. Shock was setting in at what had just happened and where she now sat. A hospital. Just like the clinic. With white walls.

Isandro came out of Zac's room for a moment, to make a quick call to Hernán and instruct him as to what time to come and pick them up in the morning, and that was when he saw her. He reeled. Rowan was staring straight ahead, her hands shaking in her lap, and she was so pale that he was surprised she was still sitting up. He quashed his immediate reflex to demand to know why she hadn't left.

'Rowan…'

No response.

'Rowan?'

No response. He moved closer and sat down. Eventually took her hands in his.

Rowan felt warmth coming from somewhere. But she was locked in a living nightmare. She knew she wasn't asleep. She was surrounded by white walls. Eventually something pierced her consciousness.

'Rowan.'

Someone was pulling her head around. Forcing her eyes to meet…blue ones. The only ones she'd ever dreamt of. The warmth of his hands was seeping through to her chilled bones and body. Like a life-giving force. And with that sanity and reality returned.

'Rowan?'

Isandro was looking at her, and it wasn't his usual impatient look. It was something different. Assessing. Speculative.

'I couldn't leave. I'll just sit out here and wait, if that's okay?'

Isandro willed down the concern rippling through him. She was in shock. Of that there was no doubt. But it was a shock so deep and raw that he'd never seen anything like it.

'Will you be okay if I leave you for a second?'

Rowan nodded, and watched as he put her hands back in her lap and walked away. She felt like calling out after him. But just as swiftly he returned and put a steaming hot cup of tea into her hands, encouraging her to drink. The tea burnt its way down her throat into her stomach and warmed her.

As he watched the colour slowly come back into her cheeks, Isandro remembered coming out onto his balcony and seeing her with her head tipped back, eyes closed…there had been something intangibly vulnerable about the lines of her body. Then he remembered the way he'd felt when he'd come to stand in front of her. All that had been on his mind was that he'd wanted to kiss her. How could he think of that at a time like this?

'How did you know what was wrong with him?'

Rowan looked at Isandro warily. 'I read about febrile convulsions in one of my baby books while I was pregnant.'

His eyes speared her, intensely blue against the white background. 'You *read* about it in a book?'

She nodded. 'They're not uncommon in children his age.'

Isandro stood up and stuck his hands in his pockets. 'And yet not I nor María knew what to do—and I am his father and she is his nanny. Dammit, that woman was meant to be the best of the best—trained to deal with anything.'

Rowan rushed automatically to María's defence. 'It's all

very well to know something in theory, but when you're faced with a child in a convulsion, turning blue… She knew what it was, Isandro, she just got a shock.'

'And yet with no training you knew exactly what to do.'

Silence hung heavy and awkward. What could she say? Sorry? She looked down at the ground and saw Isandro's feet come into her line of vision. She suddenly felt tired.

'I never said thank you.'

She looked up and shook her head, hiding her shock at his apology. 'You don't have to. I'm just glad I could help.'

And I couldn't. The words reverberated in Isandro's head. He'd never felt so impotent in all his life, never so much at a loss. He'd had to let someone else take control, and it had almost killed him.

Rowan could feel him looking at her. What was he thinking?

He stretched out a hand. 'Come on.'

She looked up. His face was inscrutable. She stood up and let him take her by the elbow. He steered her into Zac's room, where he lay sleeping, and made her sit down in the comfy chair in the corner. He took the upright chair beside Zac. She started to protest but he shushed her.

And in the half-light of the hospital room, with her son's chest rising and falling easily, Rowan let herself relax… She fought it for a long time, her eyes going from father to son, but finally she slept…

Back at the house the next day, María appeared, still looking shaken and shamefaced as she greeted them and took Zac for his morning nap.

Isandro looked at Rowan. 'You should get some rest. You can't have slept well on that chair.'

And what about you? she wanted to ask. But he'd already gone to follow María and check on Zac.

He didn't go into the office those first couple of days after the weekend, clearly still shaken by the experience. Rowan was aware of a subtle softening in his treatment of her, but knew it was far too dangerous to allow any feeling of complacency to creep in.

It was the evening of the first day that Isandro had returned to work. He'd just taken a shower and now strode towards the dining room doors for dinner, knowing that Rowan would be sitting beyond them. Inarticulate rage twinned with something much more disturbing beat in his chest. All day he'd felt a black mood engulfing him, distracting him from his work.

In the last couple of days he'd been feeling so many things, and that fear…the awful bone-numbing terror he'd felt when he'd seen Zac so defenceless…was still potent. And Rowan—the woman who had deserted them—was the one who'd been there, fulfilling her role as mother for all the world as if she'd never left, making Isandro feel blurred and ambiguous.

He came close to the door. She was dangerous. He had to remember that, despite her heroics. She had the power to do so much more harm this time. To Zac. *To him.* Isandro's eyes narrowed and his mouth thinned. She didn't have any power over *him*, it was Zac he thought of. Not himself. But still the black cloud enveloped him a little more suffocatingly as he opened the door, only to come face to face with his wife on her way out. Her eyes widened, looking up into his, scrambling his thoughts and making the rage burn more fiercely.

Rowan stared up at her husband, the breath still knocked out of her after the suddenness of his arrival. He was looking effortlessly gorgeous in a white shirt, black trousers, his hair still wet from the shower. His scent enveloped her…she fought for breath.

'Sorry… I was just… I didn't know if you were…' She

cursed herself and started again, drawing herself up straight. Immediately she knew all was not well as he glowered down at her, and couldn't begin to wonder what had precipitated it. 'I was just going to tell Julia I'd eat in the kitchen as I thought it would only be me for dinner…' She wished she had something to cling onto—and then her eyes slid treacherously to his broad chest, just inches away, and she felt heat flood her cheeks.

Finally he broke the spell and moved past her, gracefully, stealthily. And he drawled, 'There's no-one else here, Rowan… Who are you trying to impress?'

Rowan ignored him, and the silly pain in her chest at this evidence of his filthy humour. Like this he was very dangerous. She turned to follow him back into the room. 'Well, as you're here, I'll stay.'

He swept an arm out as he sat down. 'Oh please—don't stay on my account. By all means go and eat in the kitchen if you want.'

But just when she would have taken him at his word and left, she heard the door, and Julia arrived with the soup. Rowan knew it would be futile to get into a big long explanation of why she wanted to eat in the kitchen, and she didn't want to embarrass the other woman, so she sat down and busied herself with her napkin.

For the past couple of days Isandro had been somewhat civil, but that civility had obviously run its course. She avoided his eye and they ate their soup in oppressive silence. Rowan was quite tempted to just pick up her bowl and leave the room, but she was also determined not to show how he affected her.

Julia returned with the main dish, and a bottle of red wine to go along with the beef. Rowan accepted a glass and speared a morsel of the succulent meat. It almost melted on her tongue, and it had been so long since she had had anything so exquisite that she closed her eyes for a second, unconsciously savouring the taste.

When she opened them again she caught Isandro staring at her with a hard look.

'The beef is delicious.' She knew she sounded defensive.

'It's just beef.'

Rowan took a swift sip of wine. That too begged to be savoured but she stopped herself. They continued to eat in silence, and Rowan did her best not to be aware of his lean brown hands, big but graceful, as he handled his silverware. She saw him take his fork into his left hand to eat and remembered that he was left-handed. She wondered absently if Zac might have inherited that trait.

When they were finished, Isandro put his napkin down by his plate and leaned forward, cradling his wine glass in one big hand. Rowan instinctively sat back into her chair. She couldn't help but look at him. She knew her eyes were growing big and round, but couldn't help it. He filled her vision like nothing else she'd ever experienced. She felt as if he could see right through her. As if they'd gone back in time and it was one of the first times she'd seen him all over again.

Isandro watched her intently, and in that moment he felt inexplicably like pushing her, goading her into revealing…*something*. Anything. *Something that would make things easier for him to understand?* He quashed the annoying voice, and asked, 'Why did your father want to marry you off so badly that he made you a part of the deal?'

Rowan's mind seized. This was the last thing she'd expected to hear. 'Why on earth do you want to talk about that now?'

Isandro shrugged negligently, dangerously. 'Call it making conversation.'

Rowan stifled a reply. If she made a fuss, he'd know that

this was a sensitive subject for her. He was playing with her like a cat toying with a mouse, that was all. In keeping with this weird mood he was in.

She affected a shrug, much like his, and willed Julia to return. Anything to break this up and change the subject. 'I thought you knew why.'

Isandro waved a hand. 'Well, for your inheritance, I believed. But as he never made any play to get it after we got married I could never figure out why.'

Rowan was genuinely surprised. 'You thought my father wanted my inheritance?'

Isandro's gaze narrowed. 'Didn't he? He was going bankrupt. I thought he saw you as his ticket out of lifelong debt. That he was offering you up for marriage for that reason.'

Rowan's head swirled, and she put a hand to it. He had deduced *that*?

As if reading her thoughts, he added, 'It was obvious there was little affection lost between you, Rowan. Anyone could have seen that.'

She glared at him. This was getting far too close for comfort. Her own secret humiliation open for scrutiny. The fact that she'd been unwanted. Unloved. Tolerated. By her only family.

Rowan lifted her glass of wine, her hand trembling slightly, and took another sip. He was being too invasive, and yet she couldn't escape that intense regard. He would settle for nothing less than blood. This was the price she was expected to pay for wanting to be here. For leaving in the first place.

'There's something you obviously weren't aware of.'

He inclined his head, taking a slow sip of wine. 'Go on.'

Tension spiralled through Rowan. 'The truth is that my father was sick. No one knew how bad it was apart from me and his cardiologist. He had a degenerative and inoperable heart condition. It's why he lost control of his business and work. Why he looked for someone to bail him out. He wanted to save face before he died.' She shrugged minutely. 'As for me—he just wanted to see me married to a suitable husband. He had no interest in the money.'

Isandro was frowning. 'I had no idea he was ill. But why was it so important to see you married?'

Rowan could feel anger rising. Was he intent on humiliating her completely? She deliberately kept her voice as light as possible to hide the long-buried pain.

'Because he'd made a promise to my mother on her deathbed that he'd see me married to someone worthy so I'd safely inherit her fortune.' Rowan's lips thinned in self-deprecation. She'd gone inwards. 'I don't think he'd counted on it taking so long. He knew he was dying, and he needed to ensure Carmichael's safety, my inheritance. You came along and effectively killed two birds with one stone for him.'

Isandro's eyes narrowed sharply on her tense face, at her staccato words.

She smiled tightly, looking up at him briefly before looking down again, white fingers playing with her napkin. 'No doubt you were well aware that I was groomed from birth to be the perfect wife. I went to finishing school. I speak five languages. I can converse on topics as diverse as the possible extinction of the mountain gorilla in Rwanda and the theory of the butterfly effect.' She gave a little laugh then, as if revealing herself cost her nothing. 'When I was eighteen my father threw away the bi-focals I'd worn since I was nine and made me get laser eye surgery. All the better to make me a more appealing wife.'

For a long moment Isandro said nothing, and Rowan realised that her breath was coming jerkily, as if she'd just been running. And then he said softly, 'Perhaps he could see how beautiful they are.'

Rowan's heart flipped in her chest and she sent him a quick shocked look, for a second catching his eye. He coloured slightly, as if he too was shocked at his words, but then that scarily cool mask was back in place and he diverted his attention to filling his wine glass again. He was making her feel thoroughly confused. Acting so mercurial. Moody.

'So why didn't you get married before?'

Had what he'd just said about her eyes been her imagination? She shook her head faintly. 'I don't know…'

But she knew well. She thought of the men she'd been introduced to over the years. Insipid. Boring. The minute she'd seen Isandro she'd *known* him. She'd felt something deep within her spring to life, as if she'd been asleep until that moment. She hadn't believed it when her father had said he was interested in being introduced to her. But then she hadn't realised the extent of his interest in her as a trophy wife. More fool her.

That first time they'd had dinner she'd got to the restaurant before him and had sat facing away from the door. She'd cursed herself, but had been too self-conscious to get up and move. She'd waited like that, with her back so straight and tense it might have cracked, and then she had *felt* him. She could remember closing her eyes for that split second just before he'd come into her line of vision, and then he'd surprised her by asking, 'Excuse me, is this seat taken?'

She'd looked up, and he'd been smiling down at her. A half mocking smile that had been so confident, so seductive, so sure of himself. She'd blushed from that moment right through the whole meal, but amazingly the ice had been broken with his self-deprecating introduction. She'd always felt slightly guilty after he'd proposed, as if they were so completely mismatched that she'd surely taken him away from a far worthier, more soignée woman. And she'd never had to nerve to ask him why *he* hadn't married before…

She certainly didn't have the nerve to ask him that now, but she wanted his focus off her as to why she might have agreed to marry him. Her inheritance had never been important to her, and if he guessed that…

'You married me to get your foot in the English banking door. Tell me, has it worked?' She hated being reminded of a time in her life when all she'd been was a commodity to be passed off, because her father was doing no more than ticking the boxes before he died.

Isandro was calm and implacable, infuriating her with his coolness. 'Yes. You could say that,' he answered equably. 'I now control a majority share in the biggest bank in England.'

She darted him a look. 'You must be happy, then. You got what you wanted.'

He shrugged and drained his wine glass. 'Happy? I wouldn't say happy, exactly, Rowan. Satisfied, perhaps. Can you say that your frittering away of your own inheritance in these last two years has made *you* happy?'

And just like that she was brought back to the present with a mighty bump. She shook her head, not really seeing him any more. 'No. I can't say it has.'

There was a bleakness in her tone that was unmistakable. But she missed Isandro's quick glance.

Julia came in then, with coffee and dessert. Rowan thanked her for the beautiful dinner and waited till she had left. Then she put down her napkin shakily and stood up.

'I'm feeling quite tired now. I think I'll go to bed.' She felt raw and open inside. Flayed.

Isandro grabbed her wrist as she went to leave. She took a deep breath and willed the emotion out of her eyes as she turned to look down. She even managed to raise a nonchalant brow in question, even though her pulse beat crazily against his hand. She prayed he wouldn't notice.

'Tell me. Is that why you left, Rowan? Because you wanted to escape the box your father had put you in?'

No... The word ached to come out but she couldn't let it. Not yet. It was still too much to share. Especially when he was in such a dangerous mood.

So she tossed her head slightly and saw a flare of something—anger?—in Isandro's eyes. 'Yes. That's why I left.'

He gripped her hand a little harder. His mouth thinned. 'You expect me to believe that you were just a poor little rich girl, Rowan? A poor little sheltered rich girl, who ran away at the first opportunity...?'

'Yes,' she said wildly—anything just to get away from him.

'Well, I hope it was worth it, Rowan...'

It was...

She tore her eyes from his with a will she hadn't known she possessed, and snatched her hand back. She ran from the room, all pretence of insouciance gone. Once outside she walked blindly through the house and out to the garden, where she gulped in the night air. He was so right and yet so wrong. She had been exactly that. A poor, gauche little rich girl. Unbelievably naïve. Her father had done all he could to make her a biddable wife; he just hadn't counted on her chronic shyness and innate lack of grace and style thwarting his efforts.

And she hadn't run away at the first opportunity. She'd fallen stupidly in love at the first opportunity. With a man who had made her dreams of love look like a silly garish cartoon, complete with love hearts and flowers.

CHAPTER SIX

ISANDRO poured himself another glass of wine and his hand wasn't completely steady. What on earth had compelled him to rake up old ground? He'd never cared before why Rowan had married him. She just had—she'd been willing, part of a package. She'd *appeared* to be refreshingly unlike the other women of that society, which was why he'd decided to marry her as opposed to any other.

He'd clearly stated the terms of their marriage, and had thought he would be doing her a favour by making sure her father didn't get his hands on her inheritance. But he'd died soon after the wedding, and if what she'd just said was true he'd never planned on doing her out of it anyway. That bugged him now. He wasn't used to reading people wrong. His mouth thinned. And yet what had his wife turned out to be? He slugged back a gulp of wine. *A monumental thorn in his side…*

The truth was, she'd touched a protective instinct in him. From the first moment he'd seen her, and that unbelievably naïve quality about her. He'd read her outward shell of unconcern to be just that—a shell. And yet she'd played him for a fool from that first moment.

His feeling of vulnerability these last few days came back

to him and rocked him to his core. From the first moment he'd seen her again he'd viewed her as a dangerous threat. But she'd become the complete opposite… And when he'd walked into the dining room earlier all he'd seen were those huge eyes, staring at him, full of *something*. Looking at him as she'd looked at him before. When he had stupidly believed that perhaps his wife felt more for him than she had shown.

She'd asked him if he was happy. It had touched a nerve. Zac had made him happier than anything else he'd ever known, and for someone who'd meticulously planned out a life built around gaining power it had been…a revelation. A revelation that *she* was responsible for. Anger coursed through him again. He welcomed it.

More than a week had come and gone. Why wasn't she bored? Why hadn't she made an attempt to go into Seville, to the city? Why was she insisting on wearing those three tatty outfits day after day?

Was that why he'd felt compelled to goad her, to prod her? To ask her about things that had never concerned him before? To drive her to reiterate why she'd left? So that he could remember and not forget? Was he in danger of forgetting? He downed the last of the wine. He *would not* forget. And as soon as their divorce was through he would move her out of his home and they would establish her access to Zac. That was all their relationship comprised now.

When Rowan came down the stairs the following morning it was bedlam. Zac was in Isandro's arms, and he and Julia the housekeeper were trying to talk above Zac's screaming, crying. His face was puce, and Rowan guessed it was because he was being ignored. Her arms itched to take him and calm him down. It couldn't be good for him to be getting worked up so soon after the convulsion.

'What's wrong?'

Her voice seemed to cut through the mayhem and they turned to her. Even Zac halted with a hiccup. Isandro glared at her. But what had she expected after last night? They'd taken two steps forward and about three hundred back.

'María has left.'

Rowan's churning thoughts stopped dead. Much like Zac's screaming. 'María's left? But why?'

Isandro held out a note. 'Here—you seem to have a lot in common.'

Rowan ignored his barb and read the note. In effect María was saying that she felt she hadn't handled Zac's convulsion well, and now that his mother was here she didn't see that she had a role.

Rowan looked up at Isandro, speechless. He glared at her briefly, before trying to calm Zac down. He was rapidly working himself up again.

'Here—give him to me. Let me give him some breakfast. He must be hungry.'

Rowan watched as Isandro handed Zac over to Julia. She had a nervous fluttering in her belly. It was patently obvious who Isandro blamed for this. She crossed her arms.

'Isandro, I'm sorry to hear María has left—'

'Of course you are. No doubt you're loving this. Tell me, did you pay her to leave?'

Rowan's mouth dropped open inelegantly and she sputtered indignantly. 'How dare you? Of *course* I had nothing to do with her leaving. If you hired someone unprofessional enough to leave at the first sign of a crisis then you cannot blame me.'

He moved close and said silkily, 'And yet everything was running smoothly before you came back.'

His conscience pricked at that. In truth he'd begun to have his doubts about María within the last month, but he was too incensed faced with Rowan right now, her face flushed prettily with anger, to be rational or fair.

Rowan glared at him belligerently, her hands now down at her sides and curled into fists. 'Well, I did—and I'm here to stay. Are you going to accuse me of bringing on Zac's convulsion too?'

For a long second they glared at each other. His anger was tangible and awe-inspiring. Then Isandro broke the spell. He stepped back slightly and ran a hand through his hair.

'No. Of course not.' That conscience struck him again when he recalled his paralysing fear that night, and how Rowan had been the only one to retain any calm sanity. He'd just gone a step too far.

'I have to go to Kuala Lumpur today, for a three-day emergency meeting. It's something I just can't get out of. Believe me if I could I would.'

The bitterness in his tone told Rowan exactly how trapped he was feeling.

'Well, at the risk of having you jump down my throat with threats and insults, I would love the chance to take care of Zac while you're gone. You're hardly going to get a replacement nanny in such a short space of time.'

He battled to keep his face impassive, to hide his frustration. 'I know. And believe me, the only reason I'm even *considering* this is because my mother and sister are on holiday for a week. Otherwise he would stay with them...'

He ran an impatient hand through his hair again, his gesture saying it all.

'Needless to say, Rowan, I leave him here in your care with the utmost reluctance. It is only because I know your every move will be monitored and reported back to me that I do this. Hernán will remain here with you. Julia can help.'

She hitched her chin. So she was to be a virtual prisoner.

Still…it meant time alone with Zac. When she spoke her voice had lost its belligerence. 'I have no intention of going a step outside these grounds or these four walls. All I want is time with my son. I swear.'

Her eyes had turned a soft darker velvet colour, and a wealth of emotion lay in their depths even though Isandro knew instinctively that she was trying to hide it. He didn't want to know *how* he knew that. His eyes moved up and down her body, taking in the swell of her breasts under the thin material of her shirt, her worn jeans. One of those three outfits she'd been circulating since she'd arrived. Her eyes, her body, her scent threatened to scramble his thought processes…he had to push her back.

'I'll be checking in regularly.'

'I wouldn't expect anything less,' she said softly.

He looked for triumph, for any sense that she'd won a victory over him, but saw nothing of the sort. Her response, far from confirming what he'd expected, made confusion rush through him. And something else. Something very nebulous and disturbing.

Rowan watched her son sleeping. It had taken a while to put him down that night, he was too excited with the change in routine and having Rowan there every moment, as opposed to María. She was exhausted. And yet happier than she could ever remember being in her life. She bent down and lovingly tucked a lock of fallen hair back, and in doing so she was reminded of a moment once snatched, when she'd watched Isandro sleeping after they'd made love. Her heart beat so painfully that it hurt. After a long minute of just looking at Zac, she went and curled up in a chair in the corner of the room, eventually falling asleep. She didn't want to leave him for a second.

* * *

A week later Isandro stood in his study and looked out onto the lawn through the window. His return had been delayed due to a sudden crisis on the Asian stock market that had necessitated his continued presence. He'd never have gone if he'd known that might happen. He could see that Zac was working himself up into one of his increasingly frequent tantrums—a side-effect of his fast-approaching second birthday. As Rowan tried to placate him, he hit her. Isandro's insides immediately clenched in fear that she would retaliate, and he made to move—only to find himself obeying some instinct and stopping again.

As he watched he realised that Rowan wasn't reacting to the slap. Zac hit her again and Isandro winced, this time for Rowan. Again she didn't respond. She completely ignored Zac, and got up to tidy his toys away. Eventually Zac started to calm down, perplexed by this non-reaction. It made Isandro suddenly nervous of how María might have reacted in a similar situation. That niggle of conscience rose again.

After a while Zac toddled over and got Rowan's attention, and she bent down to his level. She appeared to be talking to him, and showed him where he had hit her. Isandro could see even from here that her skin was red. She seemed to be trying to explain to him that it was wrong, and then Zac threw his arms around her and kissed her. Rowan hugged him back, and Isandro felt the most curious tightening and falling feeling in his chest.

He turned away abruptly to leave the room and go outside. The feeling that seeing them had precipitated in his chest just now was terrifying with its force. Rowan Carmichael was a very real threat. He just wasn't sure which direction the threat was coming from any more.

* * *

Rowan knew he was there—that awareness gripped her. She didn't look round, though, and waited for Zac to react when he saw him. He screamed and ran towards him, and she let him go before turning around herself—only to have her heart flip over in her chest. He was so gorgeous. He was dressed in a steel-grey suit, dark tie and an impeccable shirt, and his slicked-back hair was now fast becoming tousled by small hands.

Rowan felt shy and awkward. He strolled towards her, putting Zac down as he squirmed out of his arms. She wasn't aware of how her eyes roved over him hungrily. Or of the surprised flare of response in his eyes as they were hidden by shades.

'How did it go?'

Rowan smiled wryly as she automatically checked what Zac was doing before looking up. 'Well, as it's barely two hours since you last called, there's nothing much to report.'

Isandro had to stop his reflex to return her smile. Instead he gestured to her arms, and the fading red marks from Zac's slaps. 'Zac?'

He saw her flush and quickly shake her head before stopping and smiling a little self deprecatingly. 'He's not aware of what he's doing. It's no big deal. He's just testing his boundaries. I'm trying to make him see that he can't...' She crossed her arms and put her hands around the offending marks, suddenly scared. Would he think she'd hit him back?

Her immediate reflex to protect Zac surprised him. It was almost as if she hadn't wanted him to know. 'You handled him well. I saw you.'

Her mouth opened. Something cold settled into her chest. Of course he hadn't trusted her for a second. 'You mean you spied on me?'

He shook his head and removed his shades, his eyes so blue

that they took her breath away. 'No, I just saw you out of the window before I came out.'

'Oh…' Rowan bit her lip. 'Then I'm sorry.' She looked down at Zac again. 'It's time for his nap now.'

'Why don't you put him down and then meet me in my study? I have a couple of things I'd like to discuss with you.'

Like custody…or is the divorce through already? Rowan knew rationally that it couldn't be, but it didn't stop her heart from clenching. She just nodded and scooped Zac up into her arms to bring him inside. At the last second Isandro stopped her to bend down and kiss Zac's head. His own head came close to her breasts, and Rowan could feel them respond. She closed her eyes weakly and willed him to step away. When he did, she set off on shaky legs.

A short time later Rowan knocked on Isandro's door and opened it. He was on the phone, but gestured for her to come in. She felt too antsy to sit down, so she wandered around, looking at the books on the shelves, feeling all over the place. After a week of not seeing him? How pathetic was that? Especially when he so obviously despised her.

'Sit down.'

She whirled around guiltily. She hadn't heard him terminate his conversation. She sat down warily, with her hands in her lap, and forced herself to look at him steadily.

He leant back in his big leather chair for a second before standing up. All the air seemed to have contracted in the room as Rowan watched him approach. He was jacketless and tieless again. He sat on the edge of his desk and the action pulled the material of his trousers taut over one powerful thigh. She swallowed past a dry throat and hoped she had enough self-control not to let her eyes drop.

'I've arranged for some nannies to come tomorrow for interviews.'

Rowan immediately sat up straight. 'But—'

He silenced her with a hand. 'It's not a reflection on how you have cared for Zac this last week. I'm sorry I was away for longer than intended.'

Rowan shrugged and avoided his penetrating eyes. 'It was no hardship—no work, Isandro. He's my son. I'd take care of him every day if I could.'

He quelled a quick surge of irritation. 'Well, we both know that's not how things are going to work out.'

'Yes. I know.'

He stood up then, as if restless, and paced the floor behind her. She had to turn awkwardly to look at him. He stopped and faced her, thrusting his hands into his pockets. He hadn't planned on discussing this with her now, but somehow it felt right.

'I would like it if you would sit in on the interviews. I don't want a repeat of what happened with María, and perhaps you'll be adept at seeing how qualified they are.'

Rowan stood too, to face him. She knew that it must have killed him to say that, and only his concern for Zac would have prompted it. However, this was the first time he'd accorded her anything approaching respect for being Zac's mother. It made her voice husky. 'I'd appreciate that. Thank you. But…if you feel that you're not ready to hire another nanny I'm more than happy to keep looking after Zac.'

He shook his head, negating her words. 'No. As I told you before, I won't have him become so attached to you that it will cause him undue pain when you're not around on a permanent basis. And I'm going to need another nanny more or less immediately, because you're not going to be on hand all the time.'

Rowan sat down heavily. He was sending her away. She quickly did some mental arithmetic. Perhaps she could rent a small apartment in Osuna, stay close by.

'Rowan?'

Her head jerked up. 'I'm sorry—what?' She hadn't heard a word of what he'd just said.

'I said that we're going to have to go into Seville to get you some clothes and do something with your hair.'

She stood again, feeling totally confused. 'What are you talking about?'

He frowned at her. 'What I just said. The Feria de Abril annual ball is next week, and I need you to come with me.'

Rowan shook her head again and translated out loud. 'The Festival of April ball?'

'Yes. It's one of the biggest dates in the Seville calendar.' He started pacing again. 'Last year you weren't here—that's when people started to speculate. As one of the patrons of the festival, I have to make a speech every year, and naturally there is a lot of media attention.' A flash of cynicism crossed his face. 'As we have the good fortune of your presence this year, you will accompany me and help to put wagging tongues to rest.'

Rowan automatically started to protest for many reasons—not least of which that it would be a total sham. But he silenced her, taking a hand out of his pocket and coming to stand close. Too close.

'Don't you think it's the least you could do?'

She was feeling dizzy, looking up at him. 'Well, I...of course... But won't people think it weird? And what about when it becomes apparent that we're divorcing? Won't it be obvious that something was up?'

He dismissed her words with a hand. 'I'm not concerned about that. I'm only concerned with the here and now. I'm involved in an important deal with a bank in Madrid, and their CEO has been invited. It will look good for me to show that my marriage exists.'

A week later, as Rowan got ready for the ball, she reflected on Isandro's words and shivered again. That coolness, that level of ambition, was something that had been all too familiar. Somehow, seeing him be such a good father to Zac, she'd been seduced into believing in a side of him she'd thought existed when she'd first got to know him, when she'd fallen in love with him. But that was dangerous. He'd just reminded her with his actions that he was in fact a cold-hearted businessman with no room for love or emotion in his life. Unless it was directed towards his son. She had to remember that, or she'd be the biggest fool.

The past week had flown. Isandro had taken her into Seville three days ago, on a whirlwind tour of the shops. He'd bought her a veritable wardrobe full of clothes. She'd protested, but to no avail. And when they'd come home he'd personally overseen her own tatty clothes being thrown away. She'd bristled at his high-handed behaviour but he'd ignored her again. In truth, being back in a bustling, vibrant city had been almost too much for her. She'd found the sounds, the traffic, everything a little overwhelming. She knew she'd get used to it again in time, but hadn't missed the funny looks Isandro had given her. She would have to be more careful.

She twisted in the mirror now, trying to reach the zip of the silk dress she'd chosen to wear, when she heard a voice.

'Do you need me to do that up?'

She jumped around, her heart thumping crazily, and held the gaping front of her dress in her hands. *'Excuse me!'* She hid her surprise and panic behind affront.

He strolled easily towards her and she couldn't breathe. In a black tuxedo, white shirt, white bow tie dangling undone, he was a virile picture of masculine perfection. And even though she'd seen him like this…it had been *before*. She'd been pregnant then, and later she'd had other concerns. But now every sense seemed indecently heightened. On full alert.

He took her shoulders and turned her stricken body around. She felt his hands come to the zip, pulling it up slowly, his fingers grazing her back. The hairdresser Isandro had taken her to had cut her hair into a more defined bob, and now it fell in soft waves to just below her jaw. The back of her neck was exposed, and there was something about that that made her feel intensely vulnerable…

She hadn't been able to wear a bra with the dress, and as the zip ascended now she could feel the dress being pulled up, tightening around her breasts, chafing against nipples that felt sensitive. She felt so tense that she feared she might snap in two. His hands stopped somewhere around the middle of her shoulderblades, and was it her imagination or did his fingers linger there for a second?

He turned her around again and looked her up and down, not a hint of warmth in his eyes. It helped to cool her pulse a little. That, and her mortification that her nipples must be like two hard pebbles under the material.

'And now if you could return the favour…'

Rowan looked up at him, dazed. And then she realised that he was talking about his bow tie. Her heart lurched. He'd never been able to do one up, and had always had to ask her. Those moments had been stolen guilty pleasures… She had a sudden intense memory of doing it once, her pregnant belly pressing into his body, feeling his burgeoning arousal. And then they had arrived late to the function. She really didn't think she could do what he was asking now and stay in one piece.

'Don't you have a ready-made one?' she asked with not a little desperation.

Isandro's brows snapped together. 'It's too much for you to do?'

He felt absurdly angry. He cursed himself for giving in to the impulse to come in here. He went to turn away but she caught his arm. She was looking up at him, something indefinable in those violet depths thrown into stark relief by the creaminess of her flawless skin and darker cream of her dress. For a second he felt as if he couldn't breathe.

'Wait. Let me try. It's just been a while, that's all.'

She stood in front of him and reached up to his tie. He lifted his head back automatically to help—and to avert his eyes from her gaze. Her clean, unmanufactured fragrance drifted upwards. She moved closer and Isandro could feel the soft swish of her dress against him, the fleeting glance of her body against his, but she pulled back so sharply when that happened that he looked down swiftly. She apologised.

And then he couldn't look away. Her face was flushed, her tongue protruding slightly through small even teeth as she concentrated on his tie. Her lashes were unbelievably thick and dark, so long that they cast half-moon shadows on her cheeks. He could see the dip of cleavage in the dress, the way it had pushed her breasts up slightly. They looked full and voluptuous. Once more she swayed against his body, and he had to clench his jaw so tight that he felt his teeth would snap. His erection was hard and heavy against his underwear, and he hadn't felt this hot for a woman since—

'There.' There was more than a little breathless relief in Rowan's voice as she stepped back. Tying that bow tie and remaining standing had been like her own personal Everest quest. She couldn't look up. She babbled. 'I just have to put on my shoes and get my wrap and bag and then I'm ready to—'

'Here—you're going to need these.'

Rowan glanced up quickly, and then down to where Isandro was holding her wedding ring and engagement ring in his palm.

'You still have them…' she breathed. She'd loved those rings. Her wedding band was simple platinum and her engagement ring was an antique. She'd picked it herself, a square green diamond surrounded by tiny clear diamonds in an Art Deco setting. She watched as he took her hand and held it out, efficiently slipping the rings onto her ring finger. She'd lost weight and they were looser.

'I'll have to get them re-sized.'

'What's the point?'

Rowan looked up and willed the sharp pain down. She couldn't *believe* she'd just said that. 'Of course. I wasn't thinking.'

'I'm going to look in on Zac. See you downstairs.'

When he left, Rowan took a deep, shuddering breath. That whole experience had taken more out of her than she cared to admit. She looked at the rings glinting on her finger and felt like an impostor. She cursed her big mouth again.

Checking herself quickly in the mirror, she stopped, and her hand went to touch her hair. What would Isandro's reaction have been if he'd seen her this time last year? With that thought came the uncomfortable truth. Sooner or later he would know…and what would that do?

'I like Ana-Lucía. I think we've made the right choice.'

Rowan looked at Isandro in surprise across the back of the car as they drove to the function. His helicopter had brought them to a small private airfield just outside the city. His use of 'we' had made her heart stop.

'I like her too…'

When they'd interviewed nannies the other day, for the first time they'd both agreed on something. Neither of them had liked a single one of them. They'd either been too interested in making eyes at Isandro, in the house, or in how much money they would be paid. Rowan could remember the jealous bile that had risen within her when yet another simpering blonde had cooed coquettishly at Isandro.

Then Julia had told them of a friend of hers who was looking for work. They'd met her and known immediately that she was the one. Rowan much preferred to hire someone local, and Isandro had seemed to agree.

The car was drawing to a smooth halt outside a huge, impressive Moorish building. Rowan tried to hide her awe, feeling gauche. Isandro followed her look.

'This is the Palacio de Don Pedro. It rivals the Alhambra in Granada in its preservation of drawings and carvings.'

He stepped out of the car and Rowan saw his hand stretch in to take hers. She had a moment of remembering other occasions like this, how attentive he'd been to her, making her feel secure, at ease. Emotion rose and she struggled to quell it. She took a deep breath and tried to emerge gracefully, taking his hand.

Once standing with him at the start of a red carpet, she registered the flashing bulbs of the paparazzi, numerous milling crowds, stunningly beautiful women bedecked in the finest fashions and jewels. Handsome men. But none as handsome as the man by her side. She felt momentarily stunned, in awe and fear of the obvious exclusiveness of the event.

The ball was taking place in the spectacular Salón de Embajadores. Rowan was mesmerised by the ceiling, which was a wooden dome with thousands of star patterns. She was so entranced that she gaped. When she looked down again she caught a couple of women looking at her and laughing slightly behind their hands. Her face burned crimson as the memory came back of overhearing those poisonous women in the bathroom in London. But, she reassured herself, she was different now, stronger.

'Who are they? Do you know them?'

Rowan heard Isandro's voice close to her ear and fought the urge to move her stricken eyes. She shook her head. 'No. I was taken aback by the ceiling, and I'm afraid I must have shown a little too much awe than is appropriate for such a gathering.'

He slanted a probing look down at her. Rowan looked away and took a sip of her champagne. It slid down her throat like a fizzy starburst. There were so many sensations that kept taking her unawares.

Isandro took a closer look at the women Rowan had been looking at and his heart sank. One of them was Mercedes Lopez. He hadn't been entirely honest with Rowan in his reasons for wanting to bring her along. Although it was serving him to have her here, to reaffirm his respectability after she'd made a mockery of their marriage, it was also to deter the advances of the other woman—and he could see Mercedes bearing down on them now.

They'd been lovers some years before he'd married Rowan, and with the recent notable absence of his wife she'd been agitating to resume the affair. Isandro had hoped that having Rowan by his side might send her a message. He couldn't say what it was about her that turned him off so completely now, when before she'd appealed to him, but something just did.

Unconsciously he pulled Rowan closer, and could feel her stiffen in response. It made him angry and he looked down at her, but she was looking at the other woman with wide eyes. Unaccountably, he felt protective.

Mercedes spoke in rapid and intimate Spanish as soon as she reached them, putting her arms around Isandro's neck and taking total liberties with the traditional warmth of a normal Spanish greeting. Her kisses on both cheeks lingered for far too long. And far too close to his mouth. She was beautiful, thought Rowan. And undeniably she must be his lover, for there was a wealth of intimacy that couldn't be manufactured in the woman's every sinuous movement.

She was very seductive. Tall, dark and slim. Flashing brown heavily kohled eyes, her perfect breasts moving and swaying with her dress as she gestured. Lush hips and a tiny waist.

Rowan's rising and very fledgling euphoria at being in such a beautiful place with Isandro was about to burst like a cheap balloon. She was transported back in time. The gauche outcast again. But she wouldn't feel sorry for herself. This was all a game, and she would play it as if her life depended on it. When they were divorced Isandro could do as he pleased, but right now they were married. And, God help her poor battered heart, the jealousy rising within her was about to explode.

She inserted herself expertly between Isandro and the other woman. She could feel his initial shock and held her breath momentarily. And then let it out as she felt him take her lead, moving behind her and bringing both arms around her waist so that she lay against him.

Rowan held out a hand and spoke in clipped upper-class English. 'How do you do? I'm Rowan—Isandro's wife. I don't believe we've met before?'

The other woman had to take a step backwards. A fleeting glower transformed her perfect features before it was gone. Rowan almost felt sorry for her.

'*Querida*, this is Mercedes Lopez—an old friend of mine and head of the biggest PR company in Southern Spain.'

A knife twisted in Rowan's heart. *Yeah, right.* She was glad she couldn't see Isandro's face to read what his expression might be. What little secret look he might be giving the other woman. To her intense relief, Mercedes made her excuses and left, clearly taking the hint—or else some indication from Isandro that he would see her again soon.

'Come—there are some people I'd like to introduce to you.'

And before she could dwell on the other woman, Isandro took Rowan's hand and led her through the crowd. No doubt this was the object of her role here, to be the dutiful wife, her presence proving that all was well, all was respectable.

Isandro's body still pulsed. When she'd made that cute little move to block Mercedes she'd taken him completely by surprise. And turned him on. She'd never shown any proprietary urges before.

That's because now she's back for your money and she'll do whatever it takes...

But another voice reminded him that she'd been pregnant before, and unwell for a lot of the time, not able to attend functions, so how would he know how she'd act?

Rowan found that the people Isandro had taken her to meet were genuinely nice. Other couples, also colleagues from the banking world. And none of the women were looking at Isandro as if they wanted to devour him. She was happy to speak and get used to her Spanish here, and she'd caught a warm glance from Isandro that had made her feel absurdly happy.

She was tuning in and out of the conversation a little later when one of the women took her arm, and Rowan just got her last few words. '...market crash.'

Rowan frowned apologetically. 'I'm sorry—what?'

'The European market crash of eighteen months ago...don't you remember? The absolute carnage that resulted in the economy practically sparked a global recession.'

Rowan racked her brain feverishly to try and remember if she'd heard anything. 'I'm sorry... I just don't recall...'

Isandro was frowning, giving her an intense look.

Conversation had halted around them. She knew well why she hadn't heard anything. She affected a look of delayed surprise and self-deprecation. She laughed nervously.

'Oh, *that* crash—of course I do. I'm sorry, I wasn't sure what you meant.'

The woman laughed. 'How could you be married to the man who controls finance in Europe and not remember that? You'd have to have been buried under a rock!'

Or near enough…

Rowan smiled weakly and wished the ground would swallow her up. She felt Isandro's arm tighten on her waist and looked up warily. She met that clear blue gaze tinged with ice again. He clearly hadn't been fooled by her bad acting.

And the night wasn't about to get any easier. Rowan's heart sank to her shoes when she saw who was approaching them now. Ana. Isandro's sister. Too late to escape. The crowd melted away and it was just them—and Ana and her husband.

CHAPTER SEVEN

ANA greeted Isandro and then stood back. She shared the same colouring as her brother. The same tall, lean physique. But she had her mother's eyes. Dark and hard.

'So.' She looked Rowan up and down. 'The prodigal wife returns.'

'Ana,' she heard Isandro say warningly.

His sister sent him a blistering look. 'What? You mean to tell me that after what she did to you and *to my nephew* you're just letting her waltz back in to clean you out?'

Rowan felt shaky. She could remember another conversation. One between him and his sister. That very day when she'd come home and known her life was going to change. Ana had travelled all the way from Spain to see him. Rowan had returned to hear them arguing in the sitting room. Their voices had been so raised that she hadn't been able to help herself stopping. And it was all coming back in lurid detail.

His sister's voice had been a strident shriek of indignation. 'After all the years of pain and humiliation our father put our mother through, put *us* through with that English whore of his, *you* take an English wife and now she's having your baby? *You* would do that to us?'

Isandro's own tone had sent shivers down Rowan's spine.

'Ana, nothing has changed. This is a business arrangement. The fact that she is now bearing my child is an unexpected bonus. It will save me the bother of marrying again in order to secure an heir.'

His sister's voice had lowered dangerously, reeking of suspicion. 'Are you in love with her?'

Isandro had laughed quickly, harshly. 'Of course not.'

'Then why did you sleep with her?'

Isandro's voice had turned icy. 'That is none of your business.'

'I can't imagine it was fun.' Ana's voice had been so scathing and so dripping with disdain that Rowan had felt weak. 'She's like the original ice queen.'

Their voices had got lower but no less heated for a minute, and Rowan had been too frozen with horror to move. Too shocked. Too hurt. And then Isandro's voice had risen again.

'She means nothing more to me than a means to an end. She never did; she never will. I don't *care* what our father did. That has no bearing on how I am going to live my life. I will not be dictated to by his misdeameanours, and I will certainly not be dictated to by you. She has more than fulfilled her function as my wife and you *will* accept that.'

'She's truly trapped you now, brother dear…' Ana had finished tauntingly.

Slowly Rowan became aware of her surroundings again. Ana was still standing there, hissing at Isandro. Her husband looked sheepishly apologetic beside her. Rowan felt clammy and cold.

And then Isandro was saying to Ana, *'Bastante!'*

His sister halted in mid-tirade. With a strangled sound she grabbed her husband and stalked off. Rowan felt as though she'd been punched.

Isandro turned to face her. He was shocked at how pale she looked. Her eyes were wounded. He cursed, and took her over to a quiet corner. When he almost acted on instinct and pulled her into his chest she stepped back jerkily. It made a rush of self-mockery run through him. He was getting that soft?

Rowan felt very close to the edge. Isandro had reached for her, but she knew that if he touched her she'd dissolve. And the fact that he'd almost offered to comfort her was doing even worse things to her head.

But then, as if she'd imagined it, Isandro spoke, and his tone was frigid. 'She had no right to subject you to an attack like that here.'

It helped Rowan to claw back some equilibrium. She shook her head vaguely, as if to negate what he said. He couldn't see how badly his sister had affected her. But she'd let her get to her *again*. She'd thought she'd blocked out that awful conversation, but it was still there like a brand burnt into her memory. It had been timely, though—she had to remember that. Because if she hadn't heard it when she had she'd have told him…everything. And that would have lost her the only sliver of pride and dignity she'd managed to retain.

When he asked abruptly, 'Are you ready to go back inside?' Rowan just nodded, hoping that none of the turmoil in her belly was evident on her face or in her eyes.

'Yes, of course. I just…needed a moment…the heat…'

For the rest of the evening Isandro was attentive but distant. Unbelievably cool. Perhaps seeing his sister had put things back into perspective for him? Reconfirmed his suspicions that Rowan had indeed set out to trap him? Perhaps he regretted bringing Rowan with him? Perhaps he was wishing he was with his lover?

All the way home he barely said two words to her. Thunder rumbled ominously as they got out of the car, and Rowan looked up to see rolling clouds racing across the sky, the full moon appearing and disappearing. The air was warm, but there was a storm on the horizon. A little shiver of something went down Rowan's spine. Of foreboding or something—she wasn't sure what.

Once inside the house, Isandro yanked his tie free. 'I'm having a nightcap—care to join me?'

Rowan shook her head. Not that he was even looking at her. 'No. Thank you. Goodnight.'

Something stopped her at the bottom stair and she found herself asking, just before he stepped into the drawing room, 'Is that woman your mistress?'

His broad back stopped. He turned slowly, and Rowan could have bitten her tongue. She had no right to know. She couldn't read the expression on his face.

'Why?'

She shrugged awkwardly. 'I was just wondering. You seemed...close.'

'We were lovers a long time ago. But, no, she's not my mistress.'

'Oh...well, goodnight, then.' Rowan fled before her mouth could get her into any more trouble. Even so a curious fizzing sensation filled her veins. Upstairs, she took off her shoes and checked in on Zac. He was sleeping peacefully. She straightened the covers over him, pressed a kiss to his forehead and went to her own room.

When Isandro walked into Zac's room a while later he could smell Rowan's scent lingering on the air—barely there, but *he* could smell it. He could see that she'd already tucked Zac in properly. He sat down heavily in a chair in the corner of the room and looked moodily into space for a long time.

An hour after trying to get to sleep Rowan still lay tossing and turning. Images, memories, emotions—all were swirling through her head. And most vivid of them all an image of Isandro. Tantalising and torturing her. The air in the room seemed oppressive, and she noticed that her French doors were closed. She heard another roll of thunder. She craved air, a breeze—*something*. So she got up and went to open them.

The air outside was dense, warm and unbearably heavy, redolent with the imminent storm which still hadn't hit. Rowan stepped out and looked up. Almost unbelievably drops of rain started to fall, as if they had been waiting for her cue. She stretched out a hand as they fell, heavier and heavier. Within seconds it was a torrential downpour, and jagged lightning lit up the sky.

Rowan stepped out farther, the rain drenching her in seconds. She didn't care. The moment was magical, the kind of thing she'd dreamed of over her long and hard recent months. She went down the steps and stood in her nightdress, her face tipped up to the menacing black clouds as the rain teemed down over her, plastering her hair to her head. She felt as if she were being cleansed. An intense joy filled her.

She had survived an unspeakable nightmare and she was with her son. Despite the pain of knowing Isandro wanted a divorce, she could ask for no greater happiness than that. Lifting her arms, she welcomed the rain like a benediction…

'What the hell do you think you're doing?'

Rowan dropped her arms feeling instantly silly and whirled around, her heart thumping heavily. She could barely see Isandro through the driving rain, although she could sense his tension, his irritation. He stepped closer. She could see that he was dressed in nothing but brief boxers. Rain was running in rivulets down his chest. He was already as soaked as she was.

'I…I'm standing in the rain,' she answered lamely.

'I can see that.'

He could also see that her short nightdress clung to her body like a second skin and had become translucent. His eyes dropped. He couldn't help himself. The outline of her body was clearly shaped, from her waist to her hips, down long, long legs. The dark shadow of promise between them was a tantalising invitation. The drenched material moulded to her breasts, still high and firm, their tips hard. Desire beat through his blood, hot and insistent.

'Sandro…'

He looked up. 'What did you call me?'

There was a look on her face, a yearning look that slammed into him. He'd seen that look before. His eyes were drawn to where her chest was rising and falling rapidly. He couldn't hear the rain any more. All he could hear was the beating of his heart. The beating of his pulse.

'I said Sandro.'

Isandro shook his head. He had to break out of this spell. 'No one calls me that.'

'I did,' she said simply.

A pain gripped him inside, and he was reminded of his instinctive move to comfort her earlier. 'Rowan…go back to bed.'

She moved a step closer, but not to move past him.

Feeling a surge of intense irritation, Isandro closed the distance and took her by the shoulders. 'Dammit, woman, what's wrong with you?'

Rowan was being guided by a stronger force than she could resist. It went beyond mere desire, although that was there too, burning her up so that she couldn't even feel the rain. She put her hands on his waist and felt him stiffen. She prayed it wasn't in rejection.

'Sandro…please…'

'Sandro, please *what*?' He knew he shouldn't even be engaging in dialogue, should just walk away. But there was something about her, something…different. Earnest. He felt he'd never met this woman before—or he had…but in the past, when he had believed—

'I want you.'

The three simple words exploded into his head. He tried to move but he couldn't. Her hands were on him and he wanted them on him, all over him, around him, touching him, caressing him. Her hair was plastered to her head, huge drips falling onto her shoulders. And yet some self protective instinct kept him from acting on the strongest desire he'd ever felt in his life.

'Rowan…' His voice was hoarse.

Rowan moved closer. Close enough for their bodies to touch lightly. It was as if they were both filled with attracting ions—she could feel the force of how strongly they were being pulled together. It *had* to be real. It couldn't be her imagination. The electricity in the air wasn't just coming from the sky.

'Please.'

He shook his head. But *please* sank in and reverberated through his aching body. He could see her eyes. The rain was stopping, water drops glistened on her skin, clung to her long lashes, and he wasn't strong enough to try and pull back, analyse what was going on.

With an urgent movement and a guttural moan dredged up from somewhere deep inside, Isandro put two hands around Rowan's head, cupping it, and jammed their bodies together. Then he lifted her face and met her mouth with his.

His kiss was passionate, and everything Rowan had ever dreamt of. She sank into his body, her arms wrapped around his lean waist, her breasts crushed to his torso. She couldn't believe this was really happening, but the rain and the storm had added a magical, other-worldly element to everything.

Isandro was still cradling her head, his hands around her

face, not letting her move an inch as he plundered her mouth. His tongue sought hers, tangled and danced. Rowan could feel the heat rise from a pool low in her belly. She was oblivious to the wet clothes clinging to her body, could feel only the hard evidence of Isandro's arousal against her. A fierce exulting force moved through her.

When Isandro drew back she opened eyes that felt heavy-lidded. His were dark blue, stained with desire. Without a word he bent and caught her up against him, an arm under her legs. He turned and walked swiftly to his own room, and Rowan had a quick impression of dark colours and a huge bed before he put her down in front of him. Her legs felt weak.

She looked up at him, acutely conscious now of her clinging wet nightdress, and suddenly awful reality wanted to intrude.

As if Isandro read her doubt he swiftly put out a hand and tipped her face to his, shaking his head. A hard smile touched his mouth. 'There's no going back from here.'

And before she knew what he was doing, he'd brought his hands to the top of her flimsy cotton nightdress and ripped it from neck to hem. Rowan gasped. He slipped the garment from her shoulders so that it fell behind her, and had pulled off his own briefs in a second.

They stood naked, facing each other. Before, Rowan would have been cringing from her toes upwards—but now…she was gone beyond that. For any number of reasons. Not least of which was that her desire and the memory of how he could make her feel was burning through her, making a mockery of any show of embarrassment.

She could feel raindrops from the ends of her hair falling onto her skin and shivered slightly, breaking into goose-bumps. Her breasts felt tight, aching. Her breath stalled in her throat as she watched Isandro's eyes drop, his hand come and cup one breast. Rowan's breath returned jerkily.

Isandro lazily took the weight of her breast in his hand. All of Rowan's nerve-endings were stretched and pulled, the centre of her breast screaming for his touch. He bent his head, his breath feathered, and Rowan's eyelids fluttered closed. But then, instead of taking that straining peak into his hot mouth, she felt his tongue come out and lick where a drop of rain had fallen on the upper slope.

She put her hands on his wide shoulders to steady herself. Past and present were meshed. All that remained constant were the sensations and the way he was making her feel. Rowan gave herself up to it, and deep down thanked whatever God had given her a second chance.

She opened her eyes and speared his wet hair with her hands, lifting his head and stepped right up against him. His erection was heavy, trapped between their bodies, and then she stretched up to kiss him.

Passion gripped them, overtook them. They kissed furiously. Isandro's hands roamed over Rowan's back down to her buttocks, which he cupped in his two big hands. He pulled her up and into him, so that the aching jut of his arousal was right *there*. Rowan responded, her own hands searching, seeking to touch him all over, and then she inserted a hand between them and let her fingers close enticingly along his length.

Isandro broke away, breathing harshly, eyes glittering. 'Enough.'

Rowan felt a moment of pure fear that he meant to bring her to this point only to reject her, but then he was carrying her over to the bed and laying her down. Relief swamped her. She watched as he reached for something in a drawer nearby and sheathed himself with protection. As she watched him, something inside her fell. It didn't feel right to have that barrier between them, but she couldn't speak up—not with the weight of history heavy around them. She said nothing.

Isandro, totally oblivious to the turmoil in her head, lay beside her and ran the palm of his hand down over her breasts, their tight peaks, her belly, and down farther. She opened her legs instinctively and saw something dark cross Isandro's face for an instant. Then it was gone again.

He bent and licked around the aureole of her breast for a second, his hand delving in between her legs to find that moist heat. In the same instant that he finally took one turgid nipple fully into his mouth two fingers thrust into her slickness, his thumb instantly finding the sensitive swollen bud of her desire. Rowan nearly jumped off the bed. She'd never been so aroused, so sensitive.

She moved against his hand, her eyes shut tight, the muscles in her neck corded, as Isandro suckled at her other breast. Her hips lifted in mute appeal. It wasn't enough. She wanted him inside her, where she'd dreamt of him on her long lonely nights.

'Sandro… *Sandro!*'

Isandro almost didn't hear her with the haze of desire that was clouding his brain. She was soft and silky, fragrant, and she felt like paradise on earth. And she was as responsive as he remembered—more unbelievably responsive than any other woman he'd known. That hadn't changed.

She clutched at his shoulders, twisting her hips away. Her eyes were so dark they looked black. He could see her nipples, wet from his ministrations, and he became even harder in response.

'No,' she said breathily. 'I want you inside me.'

For a moment suspended in time they just looked at each other. And then, breaking the spell, Rowan shifted herself so that she was under him. He lay between her legs. There was no hesitation. Isandro cupped one buttock, felt its peachy firmness. Her legs opened farther and, positioning himself carefully, he entered her. He watched her head go back, the way she sucked in a deep breath as she drew him in, and his head went fuzzy. It was exactly the way she'd taken him before. And he remembered every other time as if it was yesterday, as if it was now. And it *was* now.

Coming over her properly, taking his weight onto his arms, he started to thrust in and out. Rowan had released her breath and looked up as he'd withdrawn. Now she drew her legs around his waist, and Isandro couldn't stop his moan of intense pleasure when he felt himself go even deeper. He was buried so far now…

For a long time they rode the wave, eking out the pleasure until the very last moment. Rowan knew she couldn't prolong it any more. She could feel tremors building, that delicious tightness taking over, building and building. Isandro's tempo increased, sweat glistening on his skin. The raindrops were long gone—evaporated in the heat of passion—and in one second Rowan's world erupted around her into a million stars.

She'd hung suspended for a long moment, and now, as she fell, she was hardly aware of Isandro's own completion. His body jerked and pulsed in the aftermath, still thrusting sporadically, still wringing out the final pleasure, until finally he lay over her, and she held him tightly within her, within her arms.

After a long moment Isandro found the strength to move and release Rowan from him, from his weight. Pulling free of her body caused a yearning, aching feeling to surge up, and to disguise it he got up off the bed and walked into his bathroom to deal with the protection. After he'd done that, he looked at himself in the mirror of the bathroom, with the door shut firmly on the woman who lay in the bed just feet away.

The words *What the hell just happened?* reverberated in

his head, but it seemed almost too banal to try and articulate how he felt about what had just happened. All he knew was that one moment he'd been standing in front of her in the pouring rain, asking her what she was doing, and the next…the next she'd been under him, and he'd been sinking into her like a man in a desert starved of water who'd just found an oasis.

He knew what had happened. She had bewitched him. She'd heard him going into his room, *she must have*, and had gone out there in nothing but a flimsy nightdress in the rain. And she had waited, knowing that he would have heard her door open. Knowing that he would investigate. She'd sensed his vulnerability earlier, and now she had him right where she wanted him. And he…he was completely exposed in his desire for her.

Desire. That was all it was.

He straightened up. He didn't have to feel exposed, or vulnerable. Since when was desire linked to emotion for him? *Since that first night, and now tonight…* Isandro brought his fist down onto the side of the sink heavily. No, it wasn't. He could remember her breathy little *please*…as if she'd really meant it, as if she'd never even left, walked away. Well, she had.

This was nothing more than what she owed him. At some point during their marriage she'd seemed to change overnight, had turned on the ice queen act. He wasn't about to let it happen again—at least not until he'd been thoroughly satisfied. And if she thought these cute little moves were going to get her something extra from the divorce, then it would be a fine moment of revenge when she discovered it had all been in vain.

Rowan lay on the bed. She couldn't move. Aftershocks and little tremors were still pulsing through her body minutes later. Her muscles still clenched minutely. Isandro came out of the bathroom and she turned her head. She couldn't read the expression on his face, but a little shiver went down her spine. She sensed something ominous in the air.

The passion of moments before seemed to cool in seconds, and she was reminded of how wanton she'd just acted—*again*.

He came and stood beside the bed, and she didn't like what was in his eyes. She could see that he was already becoming aroused again and, despite her trepidation, she could feel herself responding. She drew her legs together, even though they wanted to open for him, and brought her arms up over her breasts, even though she felt as if she wanted to arch her back and offer them up to him again.

Confusion and fear warred with potent, aching desire. Perhaps he expected her to go? She made a move to get off the bed, but a large warm hand caught her back and pushed her down.

'Sandro…' She was breathless already. 'I thought… Do you want me to go?'

In the dim light Rowan could see a muscle flex in his jaw. 'I've no doubt that's what you had in mind, but we're not done yet.'

'I—'

But he silenced her with his mouth, bringing his whole body down beside her, trapping her with his arms, drawing a hard-muscled thigh over her legs. And she could feel his insistent erection growing, firming against her body, and knew she didn't want to go, couldn't go anywhere.

Much later the weather had calmed outside. Without looking, Rowan knew the sky would be clear. She lay encircled in Isandro's arms, her back against his chest. She felt sated, complete, and at peace for the first time in almost two years. She'd cried when they'd made love just a short while before, but she'd buried her head in Isandro's shoulder and used her moans to disguise her sobs of helpless emotion. She didn't think he'd heard them. She prayed that he hadn't.

As if sensing her wakefulness, Isandro shifted behind her. Rowan held her breath as she felt him pull his arms from around her and get out of the bed. She closed her eyes tight, and then she felt him come around and scoop her up into his arms. She couldn't pretend to be asleep. The tension in her body gave her away.

'What are you—?' Her words stopped when she saw where he was going. He was striding back towards the adjoining door, and bent to expertly open it before shouldering his way through and depositing her on her own bed, over the covers and naked. Her bedside lamp was still on from earlier, and Rowan felt ridiculously exposed in the soft light.

His eyes, cooled now after their spent passion, flickered down her body and back up, stopping suddenly at her breasts. They narrowed. Rowan felt a snake of something bad. He wasn't looking at her with desire, it was curiosity. Isandro bent down slightly, coming closer, and Rowan cowered back. But he came down on the bed and grabbed her arms, stopping her from hiding herself. With a leaden sinking feeling she knew exactly what he was looking at—what he'd missed earlier, in the dimmer light of his own room. She closed her eyes.

A scar, about two centimetres wide, in the middle of her chest, under her breasts.

'What is that?'

Rowan opened her eyes to see his finger come out to touch. She jerked her arm free, slapping his hand away. 'It's nothing. Just a scar from…' her mind worked feverishly '…a brooch pin that stabbed me.'

He looked back up to her eyes, his other hand still holding

her fast. For a moment it seemed as if he was going to question her, but then he shrugged. And that was like a slap in the face. He didn't care.

He stood lithely from the bed and looked down at her, totally at ease in his nakedness.

Rowan frowned and looked up, feeling very much at a disadvantage. His absolute distance precluded any notion she might have had of telling him exactly what that scar was, what it meant.

'Sandro…about what just—'

'Firstly, don't call me Sandro. I don't like it.'

'But I thought you liked it when we were—'

He laughed harshly. 'Before you deserted this marriage? Before you walked away from Zac? Well, that was then— this is now.'

Familiar pain lashed her inwardly. 'But what about…what about what just happened…?' She hated the uncertainty in her voice, and scrabbled to find covers to pull around her in protection.

Isandro started to walk away, his tall, lean and powerful body a vision of perfection. Gleaming golden skin stretched over hard muscles. He turned at the door.

'That's the second thing. We just slept together, that's all. It means nothing. And Rowan?' He didn't wait for an answer. 'This time I'll expect you to be willing when I want you, for however long I want you. Perhaps you'll be a better mistress than you were a wife.'

CHAPTER EIGHT

ISANDRO stood under the punishingly hot spray of the shower. His whole body was tense, his belly knotted with extreme self-reproach, self-recrimination, *self-disgust*. He had just given in to the weakest of urges—although it hadn't felt weak at the time. It had felt like a force field sweeping him in one direction only: to possess Rowan.

Savage hands spiked through his wet hair as he stood under the intense needles of spray.

Sandro. She'd called him Sandro. The only one who had ever shortened his name. She'd let it slip one day early in their marriage. He could still remember the colour that had turned her cheeks rosy at his expression. And then he had drawled laconically, 'It's fine. I like it.' And the thing was, he *had* liked it. Had thought it had meant something.

But to hear it again now was a shock. It had felt so right. A lot like how it had felt to kiss her and take her to bed. And he was sure she knew. Had *expected* to use it as some kind of trigger.

And how could he have slept with her? Not once, he had to remind himself, but twice. In quick succession. She was the worst of the worst. She had walked out on her baby. On him. Had spent the latter months of her pregnancy freezing him out. Isandro turned the shower to cold for a second, and welcomed the icy clarity the brief pain brought.

She owed him. He'd had no intention of prolonging her stay—he'd already planned on suggesting that she move either into Osuna or Seville—but *now*… Now he might keep her a while. Let this irritating passion for her burn its course. Then he'd let her go and say good riddance. Once the divorce was through, custody agreed in his favour, he would make sure he had as little to do with her as possible. Intermediaries could deal with the moments when she would take Zac, or he would be taken to her.

But with that thought came an image of Zac being shuttled from one place to the next. Isandro dismissed its poignancy immediately. It was no less than what millions of children across the globe had to deal with, and they survived. *But his child shouldn't have to just survive*…

Isandro stepped out of the shower. He told himself that his thoughts were clear. As icy as the water that had just hit his skin. But his belly was still tight, still full of *something*. It was indefinable and uncomfortable. He looked through his bathroom door at the rumpled sheets on his bed. As if to mock him, the tantalising smell of their sex, their bodies, seemed to curl around his senses, and to his dismay the recent cold punishment was forgotten and his body started to react again.

Holding onto the clarity of thought, crushing down the hard feeling in his chest and belly, Isandro strode to the adjoining door and stepped back into Rowan's room. This was all the clarity he needed—the physical kind. After all, she was just his mistress now…

'*Gracias*, Ana-Lucía.'

Rowan took Zac from his new nanny to bring him outside.

She snuggled close and buried her face in his neck, making loud kissing noises, listening to his giggles and feeling pure joy at the sound. When they got outside he started squirming, struggling to be down and running. She welcomed the distraction. Any distraction was welcome from what had happened the other night—and every night since then. Her body was tender all over, aching in secret places.

Her mind still couldn't fully cope with what was happening, what had happened. At the way she'd been so forward, so wanton that night. She'd literally begged Isandro to make love to her, when evidently he'd wanted her to leave.

And yet now he wanted her as his mistress.

And why didn't that thought fill her with the indignant horror it should? Why did it fill her with molten heat? Each night since then, when they went to bed, Isandro would either carry her from her bed to his, or come to her bed. But either way he would leave her alone afterwards. After taking her to paradise and back. Over and over again. It enflamed her, and yet made her very scared of what the fallout might be.

She put Zac down and watched him toddle off at great speed. He'd discovered the art of gardening. The art of pulling up great handfuls of earth and replanting them somewhere else— usually his clothes. She smiled and followed dutifully, but for once her son couldn't make her block everything out. Much as she tried to let him. Erotic images, wanton images, flashed through her mind with disconcerting ease and frequency.

Absently she accepted the wriggling worm that Zac proudly held out. Clearly Isandro meant to take her as he would a mistress as a form of punishment, for whatever time was left of their marriage…

She grimaced. Isandro's frequent absences during their marriage had left enough time for her to be alone and doubt everything she thought…and felt. Yet when they had spent time together those doubts had fled easily, and she'd found herself falling more and more into an abyss of vulnerable feelings. It had been so seductive. To come from the emotional wasteland her parents had offered her to being with a man as dynamic as Isandro, who'd seemed to truly *care* for her. Desire her. Especially as her pregnancy had progressed. But she'd been wrong. Perhaps not about the passion, evidently that was still there, but about everything else…

She looked at Zac helplessly. On that fateful day when she was seven months pregnant she'd found out so much…

'Papá!'

Rowan froze. How had she not sensed him arrive? And yet wasn't he in her brain all the time? With her at every moment?

She looked around to see Zac throw himself at Isandro's legs. Isandro was looking down, smiling, oblivious to the two huge mucky handprints that now adorned his pristine suit. Rowan's heart beat rapidly. He cast her a quick cool look.

'I thought I'd come home early to take Zac riding…'

Rowan stood up awkwardly and brushed off her own filthy jeans. She felt mussed and inadequate. 'Oh…okay.' Once Ana-Lucía had taken over from María, Rowan had assumed Isandro would expect her to follow the original routine. Today her time with Zac wasn't up yet, and she felt a dart of pain that Isandro could so easily wield this control.

He started to move away, with Zac, chattering nonsensically, held high in his arms. Ridiculously tears pricked her eyes, as if her heart was being wrenched from her chest just at watching them walk away.

Before they reached the house Isandro turned around, a mild look of impatience crossing his unbearably handsome features. 'Well? Aren't you coming too?'

For a stunned moment Rowan just stood there, and then

stammered out, 'Well…I thought…I mean, yes…yes, I will— if that's okay?'

He gave a curt nod, and Rowan followed them jerkily as they disappeared into the house. The sensation of being on a string was vivid and unsettling. She had to learn to control herself. Her emotions. But just for now she felt joy zinging through her at Isandro's easy invitation.

That night, as the tremors in Rowan's body started to recede and her heart resumed a normal rhythm, she prayed silently that Isandro wouldn't leave her bed just yet. Pain made her insides clench. Was this how his mistresses felt? Or was he different with them? More tender? As tender as he'd once been with her…before she'd heard his poisonous words. It was too painful to go there. She couldn't allow herself to think about that. He was here now, with her. This time was finite.

He'd pulled away to lie on his side and, craving to touch him, to stay connected, Rowan pressed her front against his back, bringing her legs up to cup his bottom, her arm around his chest. She felt him tense for a second and her mind balked. He was going to get up and go—*again*.

But after a long moment she felt him relax, and rejoiced inwardly. She heard his breaths deepen and lengthen. She felt a huge surge of emotion and pressed her lips to his broad back, as if to stifle words that threatened to spill out. She had no idea what she wanted to say, no idea what the feeling was. And then, as sleep started to claim her body and mind, she knew. She was sorry. Sorry for leaving, sorry for walking away, for not having the courage yet to explain.

Without even realising what she was doing, she pressed another kiss to his cooling skin, higher, closer to his neck, and whispered, 'Sorry, I'm so sorry…' again and again, as she kissed him softly.

Then the world was up-ended, and Isandro was out of the bed, looking down at her with scorn written all over his face before she knew which way was up.

He'd been awake...

Rowan came up on one arm and pulled the sheet around her, her heart thumping painfully as she watched Isandro reach for his trousers and pull them on.

'Sorry?' He laughed harshly. 'Sorry for what, Rowan?'

Rowan felt jittery, shaky and in shock. She had to tell him. Now. She reached for the lamp beside her bed and switched it on. Shadows danced, and the sculpted plains of Isandro's body and face were thrown into sharp relief.

But before she could get a word out Isandro was already walking away, back towards his own bedroom.

She put out a hand. 'Wait!'

He didn't stop. He ignored her and kept walking.

Rowan refused to be dissuaded and got off the bed, pulling the sheet around her and following him into his room.

He heard her and turned around, saying coldly, 'I've had enough for tonight. Please leave.'

Rowan did her best to ignore the shaft of pure ice and pain. 'Please, I need to tell you...to explain—'

He advanced, and she backed away despite her intentions. He was just too big, too intimidating and too *male*. Her body throbbed as if on cue.

'Explanations are not something I'm interested in, Rowan. Explanations are for people who are interested in hearing what the other has to say. My interest where you're concerned is confined to the bedroom and to how I'm going to make sure you don't get a minute's access to Zac that isn't approved by me.'

He took her in: flushed, tousled, sexy. His face tightened. He made a split-second knee-jerk reaction decision. He knew he was doing it, and his weakness made his voice unbearably harsh. 'In fact, I've been thinking. The divorce is underway, and I think you've spent enough time here. I've been more than generous where Zac is concerned, but the time has come for you to leave.'

Rowan's head reeled. They seemed to have gone from zero to a thousand in emotional voltage in a nanosecond.

'Isandro—'

'I see *Sandro* has gone out of the window.' He mimicked her voice in a cruel parody of passion. '"Sandro, I want you so much. Sandro I need you—"'

'Stop it!' Rowan cried out, with such vehemence that he did. He was flaying her heart with a whip, shredding it to pieces, and it was in that moment that she knew for certain that she'd fallen for him all over again—had never really stopped loving him. Otherwise he wouldn't have the power to hurt her so deeply.

'All I want is to tell you where I've been since that day, Isandro. It's not easy for me to tell you—' *Especially when you're like this...*

'And I know why.' His arms were crossed, a sneer on his face.

'Why?' she asked, as if she couldn't already guess the answer.

'Because you've had to try and figure out how to make yourself look as sympathetic as possible.'

He started to walk around her then, making her dizzy, but he wouldn't stop, so she gritted her teeth and stood still.

'Do you need me to show you the note again, Rowan? I still have it downstairs.'

She hid a shudder. She could still remember writing it, the bile that had been in her throat as she did, the unbelievable pain in her heart.

She shook her head, feeling sick. 'No...I don't need to see it.'

'Because you were very clear. "I'm not ready to be a wife

and mother. I have things I want to do, things I want to see…"
Is that about right? Forgive me, I might have forgotten the
actual wording.'

She turned to try and face him, but he eluded her efforts.

'Isandro, I know how the note looked. But believe me—I
only wrote it because I never expected to see you or Zac again.'

He stopped and turned to face her, and she took a step back.
He was livid. She heard her words reverberate and winced.
They had come out all wrong. Well, right *and* wrong.

'No—wait. It's not like that—'

'No, I'm sure it's not. But your inheritance running out and
you not finding another willing sucker drove you back here
to a cushy prenup, using Zac, the convenient ace up your
sleeve, along the way to curry favour.'

Rowan opened her mouth but nothing came out, and in any
case Isandro wasn't finished.

He came and stood right in front of her. Worse than
anything, he just looked emotionless now. 'You've been dead
to me since you left, Rowan, dead to Zac. And in many ways
I think it might have been preferable if you had died, or at least
stayed away.'

He couldn't know what he was saying. He couldn't
possibly have any clue as to how cruelly close to home those
words were. Rowan comforted herself with that as she stood
there and felt ice trickle into her blood and her heart freezing.
There was so much meaning, so much hate in those words that
she had to get away from him. Before he could reduce her
completely. She had thought she'd been to hell and back
already, but this was coming a close second.

She looked somewhere in his vague direction. 'I agree
with you about moving out. I had already thought of perhaps
renting somewhere in Osuna. I'll get on to it tomorrow.'

And then she turned and went back into her room, shutting

the door softly behind her. In a moment of black parody her sheet caught in the door and she couldn't move forward. Loath to open the door again, to face Isandro's wrath and very evident self-disgust, she dropped the sheet and went straight to her bathroom. She pulled on a robe and locked the door, then sank to the floor in the dark and dropped her head to her knees, wanting to curl up into as small a ball as possible. No matter how much she tried she couldn't stop Isandro's words going round and round. And with them was another word: *fool...fool...*

CHAPTER NINE

ISANDRO looked at the piece of sheet caught under the door and waited impatiently for Rowan to open the door again and take it out. But she didn't. What was she doing? Just standing there? His irritation and anger levels had been finally cooling somewhat, but threatened to spike again now. He went and opened the door, only to find the crumpled sheet on the floor and the room bathed in soft light which jarred with his nerves.

The bed was empty. Where had she gone? He trod softly to the bathroom door and was about to knock, not even sure why he had felt compelled to come into the room at all, when he heard a soft noise. A keening sound like he'd never heard in his life. It made the hairs on the back of his neck stand up, his blood run cold.

His hand was still raised to knock on the door. His mouth opened but he couldn't articulate her name. A louder sound came now, and it was so primal, so *private*, that Isandro backed away, his hand dropping slowly. An image came into his head of her face when he had told her that she should have stayed away…and the other thing he'd said, about her dying.

He'd heard the words come out of his mouth and had wanted to swallow them back. But it had been too late, and before he'd been able to assess the consequences of them, of how he might have revealed himself, he'd been diverted by her reaction. She'd gone stony silent, pale as the sheet around her, her eyes dimming. She'd retreated back into the cool shell he remembered so well. It was as if what he'd said had really *hurt* her. And yet if she was nothing but a scheming, gold-digging heiress, looking to cash in on her marriage, wouldn't she have just tried to cajole him back into bed? She could have done it easily.

He couldn't disguise his shaming attraction. It burned like nothing he'd ever experienced, and surpassed even what had left him a little shell shocked after the explosive revelation of their wedding night.

But she wasn't cajoling him back into bed. She was in her dark bathroom, making the kind of sound that Isandro knew he'd never forget. But he couldn't go in there. He knew instinctively that she believed she was without witnesses, and to intrude would be unthinkable. So he left, his mind racing as to what she was up to now, what this might mean. Everything was up-ended all over again—that clarity as laughably elusive as ever.

For a couple of days Rowan studiously avoided Isandro, still raw and hurting after their row. He made no attempt to take her to bed again, or to come to her bed. He hadn't mentioned her moving out again but Rowan had made contact with an agent in Osuna and it hung in the air around them ominously. But that evening at dinner, after a painfully stilted conversation, she was surprised when he said that she and Zac should go to Seville the following day for a visit. For the first time in two days Rowan felt a spark within her erupt. She said yes, not knowing if his offer was as benign as it sounded. When he asked Rowan to come into his study after dinner she followed warily, keeping her eyes averted from the sheer force of his physique in worn jeans and a light sweater.

She stood resolutely behind a chair. Her body was feeling weak. A hunger was starting to rage through her blood at his proximity, but evidently Isandro's passion had burnt itself out. And no way would she be revealing her own vulnerability to him.

She watched as he opened his drawer and plucked something small and shiny out. He came around the desk and handed it to her.

'Here—it's a mobile phone.'

She looked at it, confused. 'But I have my own phone. I don't need yours.'

'You do need it if you're going out on your own and taking my son with you.'

Her eyes met his. 'He's my son too.'

His jaw clenched. 'This phone has all my numbers stored in case something should happen.'

'What on earth could happen?'

'You just need to be careful. We were featured extensively in the papers after that night in Seville. People know you're back on the scene. Change like that makes me and Zac and you vulnerable.'

Rowan felt a shiver of fear. She wasn't stupid. Of course a man as wealthy as Isandro could be a target for all sorts. She still ignored the phone.

'We don't have to go into Seville—'

Irritation shot through Isandro. Couldn't she see he was doing this for *her*? The fact was, ever since he'd heard her crying the other night and witnessed her withdrawing into herself, he'd been…frightened. He wanted a reaction—wanted to make her do something. *Wanted to see her during the day now as well as the night.* His body throbbed uncomfortably and he tried not to let his eyes roam over her hungrily as she stood in front of him.

He was so distracted that he barely noticed when she

finally accepted the phone. 'I still don't see how it's different to my own.'

Isandro shook his head. 'If anything happens just speed-dial me on number one. But I'll send Hernán with you too, so I'm sure you'll be safe.'

Rowan turned the phone over and back. She looked up for a second before she left. There was an intensity in his eyes that she couldn't fathom and which made her legs weak. She had to get out of there. She turned to walk out, but at the door he called her.

She turned back.

'I'll see you at the office. The girls will be looking forward to seeing Zac.'

A moment of pure exhilaration gripped her at his banal words, for all the world as if this was normal, as if they were a happily married couple discussing plans for the next day. And then just as swiftly Rowan felt that everything was crystal-clear. How could she have been so stupid? Anger rose, swift and bright. She walked back into the room, clutching the phone.

She held it out. 'This isn't about security at all, is it?'

Isandro had the gall to look nonplussed.

'You're afraid I'll try to run with Zac if you give me the slightest chance, aren't you? You're testing me.'

Two spots of colour were high on her cheeks and she was shaking. Isandro was genuinely taken aback. He hadn't thought of that for a second, and now he felt stupid for *not* doing so. Because clearly it was uppermost in *her* mind. He advanced around the desk.

'Is it cramping your style for me to know where you are at every moment of your journey?'

Rowan wanted to throw the phone back in his face. She could feel its imprint in her palm. She longed to tell him she didn't want to go to Seville, but she knew this was an important step in the process of making him trust her with Zac. Still words slipped out, helplessly. 'When will you just trust that I have only the best intentions where Zac in concerned?'

His eyes glittered down at her, a stormy blue. 'Oh, maybe on the twelfth of never.'

Rowan backed away to leave again. 'Send an army with us if you wish, Isandro. I don't care.'

But she did, she knew, as she left and went upstairs.

Isandro went and sat down behind his desk, driving a hand through his hair. Even as she had been standing there, mocking him for his own lack of suspicion, he'd been aware of her. Aware of her body, of the rise and fall of those soft breasts under her shirt. He wanted her. Mistress or wife. In his bed. And he hated to admit that he'd been ridiculously comforted to see a spark return to her eyes after two days in which her only animation had been inspired by Zac.

He'd vowed after the other night not to touch her again, but he knew that might be taking his will a step too far. The woman was running rings around him and she didn't even know it. But if she did, or if she suspected for a second…

His phone rang and he answered curtly. He heard his assistant's voice. 'What…? Nothing?' His hand spiked through his hair again. 'Yes, I want you to keep looking. Leave no stone unturned. She can't have just disappeared off the face of the earth.'

He slammed down the phone. He also hated this impulse to find out for himself exactly where she had been all this time. Forewarned was forearmed, he told himself. It was clear she'd been trying to tell him, but he would not listen to her lies before he had the truth in his own hands.

* * *

The next day Rowan looked at the phone for a long time. It seemed to shine up at her malevolently. But at the last second she threw it into Zac's bag of necessities. She knew it would be childish to leave it behind, and she had no doubt that Isandro would be most likely checking up on her.

She couldn't help a frisson of excitement as she settled Zac into the baby seat of the Jeep. The thought of Seville didn't scare her any more; she was feeling so much stronger these days. They loaded up—she in the back with Zac and Hernán driving. They waved goodbye to Ana-Lucía, who was on the steps.

Then Rowan was distracted, because Zac was grouchy and demanding attention. She tended to him for a few minutes, digging out water and a biscuit, so she didn't see Hernán slowing down or coming to a stop until he had, about a mile outside the small town.

She looked around his seat and asked in Spanish, 'Everything okay?'

'No problem. A car has broken down and I recognise it as my cousin's. I'll just check to see if he's okay…'

She looked back through the rear window. The broken down car was some distance behind them. Hernán had obviously passed it before he'd seen it. She made funny faces and played with Zac, and then cast another half-interested look back to the other car.

What she saw made her blood run cold and her heart stop. As she watched Hernán approach the car, a man stepped out from under the hood with a wrench and hit him on the head. It was so unbelievable and so fantastic that Rowan literally did not believe her eyes—not even when she saw another man emerge from the back of the car. Hernán fell to the ground, and the man with the wrench approached her in the Jeep.

She was stuck, couldn't move, but finally, when he was mere seconds away and she saw the flesh-coloured balaclava, she jerked into action and fumbled for the locks on the doors. There was only one thought in her head: *Zac*.

She was too late. The door on Rowan's side was pulled open, and the man grabbed her and pulled her out so fast and with such violence that her head spun. He was shouting at her in Spanish, but she couldn't make any sense of it. Then the other man arrived. He grabbed her too, and said roughly, '*Habla español?*'

She shook her head again, to try and clear it. He took that as a no.

'*Stupido*—Hernán said she's English. She doesn't speak Spanish. Get the kid.'

Rowan forced her mind to clear. Sheer primal protectiveness came to the fore and gave her courage. She made for the other side of the Jeep and Zac, babbling in English. She knew she'd have an advantage if they thought she didn't understand them.

She got to the door before they did. She ranted in English. It worked. The two men looked at her, and then she heard them say, 'Let *her* take the kid. What does it matter? I don't want to hold a screaming brat, do you?'

The other one grunted and gestured for Rowan to open the door. She did. Her hands were shaking so much that it took an age to undo Zac's straps and lift him out. She grabbed his bag too, in a moment of blinding clarity. Zac sensed the tension immediately and started to whimper.

The men shoved her roughly and moved her towards the other car. Everything happened in terrifying slow motion, and yet conversely so fast that before Rowan knew it one of the men had frisked her and she was sitting in the back of the car, arms firmly wrapped around Zac. Rowan's flesh still crawled from where the man had felt her bottom.

One of them put a secure blindfold over her eyes. They then got into the front and started the engine, pulling away with a screech of tyres. She couldn't let herself be scared. Think, think, *think*. She repeated the words like a mantra. The phone. She had to find it and call Isandro somehow. If she didn't it would be hours before the alarm might be raised. She just prayed that it wouldn't ring. She shushed and settled Zac securely into her chest, and then with a free hand started to feel for the bag. She found it—and felt a big hand over hers, stopping her. Her heart thudded painfully.

'Water!' she said urgently. 'Water for my baby.'

'It's okay—she just wants water. Let her get it.'

The hand left hers and Rowan searched. She found the water instantly, and then searched for the phone. About to give up hope, and fearful that the man would take the bag and get the water himself, finally she found it. She could have wept with relief. It was so small she could tuck it into her palm behind the bottle.

When she could feel that Zac had taken the bottle in his hands himself, she surreptitiously moved her hand behind him, to hide what she was doing. The men were talking now, arguing. Rowan used their preoccupation. She felt for where she thought the first digit would be. Then she pressed it, and racked her brain for where the call button had been.

With no idea if she was doing anything right, she pressed a button just as she felt the car slowing, then turning onto what she guessed was a motorway as their speed duly increased. She used the moment to throw the phone back into the baby bag. Was it her imagination or had she heard someone's voice, distant but there? Rowan knew that if she had got through to Isandro this might be her only chance, so she leant forward and said loudly in Spanish, 'Why are you kidnapping us? Where are you taking us? Why did you knock Hernán out? He could be badly hurt—you should call an ambulance…'

There was silence for a second, and then mayhem. She sensed the blow before it came, but it still snapped her head sideways. 'She speaks Spanish!'

Zac started to cry again, and Rowan calmed him down, knowing that their patience was less than thin.

One of them shouted back, 'We're taking you away for a while, to give your rich husband time to think about how much you're worth. And once we have you…' He mentioned in lurid detail what they would do to her, and Rowan blanked her mind. It was the only way. Thankfully Zac seemed to have quietened; she could feel him heavy against her chest. Tears pricked her eyes. She couldn't believe this. If anything happened to Zac… She vowed that it wouldn't. They would have to step over her dead body first.

After what seemed like hours over potholed roads they stopped. Rowan knew they'd been climbing in altitude because her ears had popped. One of the men pulled her from the car and ripped off her blindfold. She blinked painfully. Zac was a dead weight, mercifully asleep.

'No harm you seeing where we are now, because, *querida*, it's too remote to worry about.'

He shoved her in front of him towards a small stone shack. It was up on the top of a mountain, and there was literally nothing else in sight but craggy peaks.

Despair rose. The shack was windowless and cold and damp. She was pushed into a room and the baby bag hurled after her. Alone at last, Rowan put Zac down on a mattress and rummaged through the bag. She found the phone and the screen was smashed. It must have happened when the bag had hit the ground.

She busied herself getting a blanket for Zac to lie on. He was waking up again, groggy and cranky. She only had milk and baby snacks. She gave him another biscuit, which kept him occupied for a while, and then a bottle. She changed his nappy, trying to make things as normal as possible.

But after that his energy was boundless, and she couldn't blame him after being in the car and asleep for most of the day. She tried to encourage him to play quietly, but of course he had no understanding of the situation they were in.

He marched to the door and tried to reach up to open it, crying out when he couldn't. Rowan had been searching in vain for any means of escape, and darted forward just as the door opened, knocking Zac backwards. He started to cry, and the man bent down, his huge hand heading straight for Zac's head.

'No!' Rowan screamed, and pulled Zac back out of danger. She straightened up, breathing harshly, and had no warning of the hand that now came her way, cracking across her face. She felt her lip split and staggered back. The man went for Zac again, but like a tigress Rowan made a leap and caught Zac up into her chest.

Her head was ringing and she could taste blood. 'Don't *touch* him.'

The man stepped forward, but Rowan stood her ground.

He stopped then for a second, as if slightly confused. 'If I hear him so much as breathe I'll throw him down the mountain.'

He left the room and, shaking, Rowan went to the mattress and sat down, taking Zac with her. He was mercifully quiet, his eyes huge as he looked at her and her cut mouth. He put out a finger and pointed. Rowan tried to smile, but pain lanced her head. She spoke softly to try and reassure him, and got a tissue to try to stem the blood coming from her lip.

Losing all sense of time and place in the dim light, Rowan found her eyes closing. Zac had fallen asleep against her chest, and she wrapped his blanket around him to keep him warm. Her head kept nodding, and when she jerked upright some time later and found they were in the same position she had no idea of how much time had passed. She was so stiff that her legs had gone numb, her arms had pins and needles.

She came fully awake in an instant, though, when she sensed something outside. A movement, *something*… Zac woke too, and whimpered. Immediately Rowan was on her guard and stood up on wobbly legs, holding Zac tight within his blanket against her.

This was it. She knew it. They were going to try to take Zac from her and then— Her mind went blank with the horror of what was about to come.

The door opened, light streaming in from a flashlight and Rowan blinked. 'You will have to kill me to get to my son. My husband is on his way, and he knows exactly what—'

'*Rowan? Mi Dios*, what have they done to you?'

Rowan thought she was hearing things. She had to be making it up. It couldn't possibly be—

'Sandro…?'

'*Sí.* Yes. It's me.' His voice didn't sound like him. She couldn't trust it. It couldn't be possible. He came into the room, and more lights blazed behind him. Rowan felt disembodied, wasn't sure if she was standing or sitting or lying down. All she was aware of was Zac in her arms.

And then he stood in front of her. Tall and dark in the light, and so handsome and vital and *real*. If it was a hallucination then she could die happy right now.

CHAPTER TEN

THE adrenalin was still pumping through Isandro's body, and the metallic taste of fear was still in his mouth. When he'd opened that door all he'd seen had been two huge pairs of violet eyes. And such determination and fearlessness in Rowan's. For a second the emotion coursing through him made him stop. He couldn't actually touch them yet because he was shaking so much.

Rowan finally allowed the relief in, the reality, and then all the other emotions she'd been suppressing surged up. 'Sandro, I'm so sorry. I shouldn't have said I'd go to Seville. If we hadn't been going then this wouldn't have happened. Zac should have been at home. I could have gone on my own. You were right. I never should have come back in the first place. It's my fault—'

Isandro's heart clenched painfully. It had been *his* suggestion, his fault. And yet she was blaming herself. 'Shh, Rowan, it's okay. Give Zac to me.'

She stopped, feeling her mouth trembling, her limbs starting to shake. She knew she had to let go of Zac but she just *couldn't*. She tried, but it was as if her arms were welded across him, holding him so tight. A sob broke free. 'I can't— I can't let him go.'

'You can. Here…'

She felt Isandro put his hands over hers and warmth seemed to seep through her chilled skin. She felt Zac move instinctively towards his father, and somehow, finally, she was able to relax her arms from their death grip.

He took Zac and held him close for a long moment, and then she watched incredulously as he handed him to someone behind him. Then he turned to her and took her hands in his again. 'Do you think you can walk?'

She nodded, feeling slightly removed from everything. Why wasn't he just leaving now that Zac was okay?

'Of course—I'm fine—' She took a step and her legs promptly gave way, but as if he'd been expecting it Isandro caught her and scooped her up into his arms.

Rowan's mouth felt funny, and as they came out into the other room her eyes blinked in the intense light. Isandro was looking at her. At her mouth.

'What happened?'

An ugly voice came from beside the door. 'I hit her when your brat wouldn't shut up.'

Rowan tensed immediately in reaction to the horribly familiar voice and knew the two men were there, albeit probably tied up. She felt Isandro tense too. But without a word he walked outside and gently placed her in the back of a warmed Jeep, beside Zac, who was in a baby seat being tended to by a female police officer who smiled kindly at Rowan.

Rowan vaguely took in all the police, the flashing lights. She heard a scuffle and then Isandro was walking back out and cradling his hand. He sat into the front passenger side of the Jeep and the driver expertly swung them around to drive away.

Rowan knew he'd gone back in there and hit the man, and she felt glad. Because she would have hit him herself if she'd had the strength.

Sleep was rising to claim her. She couldn't fight it, but she had to ask, 'Hernán? How is Hernán?'

Isandro turned around, but he was a blur in her vision. 'He's in the hospital. He's going to be fine, thanks to you and the phone…'

His voice got further and further away…

Rowan woke as she was being carried into the house. It took a minute for things to seep into her consciousness, and when they did she tensed rigid. 'Zac—where's Zac? Who has him? Where—?'

'He's fine. He's with Ana-Lucía. She's feeding him and bathing him.'

Rowan struggled to be free from Isandro's arms. 'I don't believe you. I need to see him.'

His arms tightened around her. 'Rowan, relax. He's fine. I need to clean that cut on your lip, and then you need to eat too.'

Rowan forced herself to relax and let him carry her. It felt so good to be held like this, against his broad chest. She felt protected and cherished and safe. It was dangerous.

He let her drop outside his door, let her legs touch the ground. Rowan took a step. They felt shaky, but okay. He held her hand and she followed him into his room and to the bathroom. He made her sit down on the toilet. Then he rummaged for a first aid kit and pulled it down. Coming onto his haunches in front of her, he took out cotton wool and antiseptic. He dabbed at her lip and she sucked in a breath at the sharp pain. She noticed then that she was filthy. Dust and grime everywhere. Blood smeared on her T-shirt.

Isandro cast her a glance. 'You must have been freezing. It was almost zero degrees up there, you were so high.'

Rowan shook her head. She genuinely hadn't felt the cold. 'I don't…I didn't feel it. Had to keep the blanket on Zac in case he got cold…' Her teeth started chattering then, as if his words had unlocked something she'd been clinging onto, some control. She valiantly tried to hide it.

A look crossed Isandro's face, and then he said, 'I'll be back in a second.'

He got up and left the room, and she heard him go out into the corridor. She stood up shakily and looked at herself in the mirror. She was white, with two bright red spots in her cheeks. Her eyes were overbright too. A lurid cut snaked out from the side of her lip and throbbed painfully. Efficiently she started to pack away the first aid kit.

'Leave it—I'll do that. Sit down.'

'Oh.' Rowan hadn't heard him come back. She sat down and watched as he held out a tumbler. The smell of brandy hit her nostrils as he held it up to the side of her mouth that wasn't split, making her drink some. She didn't argue; the shivering was still there. The liquid burnt its way down her throat and she coughed slightly, but she could feel it going to work, warming her insides, calming the uncontrollable shivering.

'I'm sorry—this would never have happened if… I can't believe I put Zac in such danger…'

Isandro crouched down in front of her again and said sternly, 'Stop that. It could have happened just as easily with me.'

Rowan blanched. The thought of Isandro and Zac being kidnapped was more horrific to her than the thought of what those men might have done to her.

She shook her head to clear the fear, the awful image. 'Still, they went for me because they knew—'

He put a finger to her lips. 'Hush. They went for you because one of them was Hernán's cousin. He took advantage of knowing Hernán's movements and thought he'd try and be smart, make a quick buck. They were nothing but stupid thugs. You were so brave, *mi querida*.'

She shook her head, confused by the warmth in his eyes, the endearment. 'No, I was scared.'

'But you protected Zac; you were strong. I never knew you were that strong…'

He came up between her legs and placed his mouth gently over hers, his lips feathering across hers in a benediction, a healing kiss. Rowan wanted to sink into him, into the kiss, wanted to take what he was offering, to take the very essence of him, make it her own. She knew that they had just been through something extraordinary and had survived. He was just grateful, that was all. She knew all about moments like this, surviving. The euphoria would soon fade. His resentment would still be there somewhere, under the surface.

She pulled away gently, even though it felt like the hardest thing she'd ever done. She smiled awkwardly and her lip throbbed. She felt dirty. 'I think I'd like to have a shower…'

After a moment he stepped up and back, a blank expression replacing the warmth.

'Of course. Do you need a hand?'

'No, thanks,' Rowan said hurriedly, too hurriedly. The thought of him being around her when she felt so vulnerable was emotional suicide.

She made her way back to her own room and into the bathroom. She stood under the hot spray and scrubbed at her skin, scrubbing at any part those animals had touched. When she finally felt clean she got out. Throwing on a robe and rubbing her hair dry, she stepped back into her room.

Almost immediately, as if he'd been listening for movement, their adjoining door opened and Isandro walked in. 'Dinner. You must eat.'

Rowan knew better than to argue, and she followed him out of the room and down to the kitchen, where a steaming plate of stew waited for her with some crusty bread. Her stomach rumbled, and Isandro rested back against the sink as she sat and ate under his supervision.

'Do you want some wine?'

Rowan shook her head. The effects of the brandy were already going to her head. 'Just some water, please.'

A full glass materialised in seconds. Rowan glanced at Isandro, seriously nonplussed to see this side of him. He turned from the sink and caught her looking. She blushed and covered it up.

'How long were we…? I mean, when did you know…?'

'You don't know?'

She shook her head. 'I was blindfolded, and we drove for a long time. I don't wear a watch and one of the men threw down Zac's bag and the phone smashed.' She had to repress a shudder.

Isandro came and sat down, as if sensing her need to be near someone. 'My phone rang this morning, when you dialled it, and we found you at six p.m. They'd taken you out to a remote part of the national park. It lies to the east of here. They had you for about eight hours. If you hadn't called and raised the alarm it would have been much later, possibly even tomorrow. We lost your navigation signal when you entered the park…'

Rowan shivered again as it all came back to her. She stood abruptly, her chair sounding harsh on the tiled floor. The panic was returning. 'I need to see Zac. I have to know that he's—'

Isandro came around the table. 'He's fine, Rowan.'

'I don't care—I need to see him.'

She started out of the room and Isandro was right behind her. She had the most irrational fear that was galvanising her movements, making them jerky. She walked to Zac's room and pushed open the door, her heart thumping. Ana-Lucía turned around from where she was tucking him in. He was fast asleep. Rowan sagged against the door. Tears of proper relief stung her eyes.

She saw Ana-Lucía send a concerned look over her head to Isandro, and felt him turn her around and propel her to her room.

'See? He's fine. Now you need to sleep too.'

Isandro knew his voice sounded husky with suppressed emotion. Rowan looked up at him and her eyes were bright. Seeing her here, with Zac, when he'd thought…he'd feared the worst. He couldn't think of that fear, couldn't let it rise again. It had almost undone him earlier. He could still feel his fist smashing into that man's face, the police pulling him back, and knew he might have gone a lot further. He would have put Zac in danger because he wouldn't have been able to control himself, but Rowan had exhibited calm and control and had put Zac first every step of the way.

When his phone had rung in the middle of a meeting he'd almost let it go to message, but he'd somehow known it was her. He'd picked it up, and then he'd realised what he was listening to. He could still feel the acrid fear and panic that had seized his innards.

His churning thoughts halted as Rowan stepped away from him to go into her room. 'Will you be okay?'

Rowan looked at him. She knew she should say yes, that she'd be fine, thanks, and goodnight, but her mouth wouldn't work. *Just for tonight. Please just let me have tonight, and tomorrow I'll get on with the rest of my life.*

She faced him and lifted her chin slightly. 'Would you…? I mean I know that you don't—that we aren't—'

She stopped. She couldn't even string two words together. She turned in mortification and shame but felt Isandro tug her back.

'Do you want to sleep with me?'

Colour scorched her cheeks. She couldn't look up. 'Not like that…but, yes, please. I don't want to be on my own.'

Without a word Isandro took her by the hand and led her along the hall to his door and into his room. In the dim light he undid the belt on her robe. She started to protest that she had nothing on underneath, but he just shushed her. He slipped the robe from her shoulders and then stepped out of his own clothes until they were both naked.

He brought her over to the bed and waited till she was in, then he got in the other side. Rowan thought he was just going to let her lie alone, but immediately she felt the heat and hardness of his body as he pulled her in close to his chest, his legs cupping her bottom. She could feel his body stirring against hers and she shifted slightly.

He pulled her closer, a possessive arm around her belly, and whispered in her ear. 'It's okay. It's something I can't help with you so close. Go to sleep, Rowan.'

Heat and pleasure and warmth and safety fizzed through Rowan's veins. She finally allowed herself to relax back against Isandro's chest. Let his warmth and the strength of his body seep into her bones and skin. She'd said she hadn't felt cold earlier, and she hadn't. But now she realised that she had. She'd just blocked it out. It was a coldness the like of which she hoped she'd never experience again. It was the coldness of hopelessness, and even throughout everything she'd been through before she'd not felt it until today.

She knew she must have slept for a while, because when she woke a little later she could feel Isandro's arm heavier around her. More of a dead weight. She felt in that moment as if she could quite happily lie like that for ever.

Emboldened by knowing that Isandro was asleep, she ran her hand lightly up and down his arm, leaving her hand to rest over his. It felt strong and big, the fingers long and capable. Vibrant and alive. She turned her head to try and see his sleeping face and he moved. She tensed. She was going to break the spell. He'd wake, forget everything that had happened, wonder what on earth she was doing in his bed…

Rowan froze. Isandro moved again and she could feel him against her bottom. He wasn't as hard as before, but he was coming back to life. Her cheeks grew warm in the dark as his hand started to move lazily on her belly, upwards, to the curve of her breast. He cupped it lightly.

Rowan's breath stopped. She sucked her belly in as his hand moved up and over her breast fully, trapping her hardening nipple between two fingers, squeezing gently. There was no point trying to play dumb. Her whole body was humming, singing, and she could feel him move restlessly against her, now rock-hard and *big*.

About to say *Sandro*, she stopped, remembering his mocking words from the other night. 'Isandro…?'

'Shh.'

He pressed kisses all down the back of her neck onto her shoulder. Fire was raging between her legs and Rowan could feel herself parting them in a tacit plea. Isandro took his hand from her breast and smoothed it down in a sensual journey, over the indent of her waist and out to her hip, down her thigh and back up, before going between her legs and opening her up to him. She felt him guide himself between her thighs, seeking the hot, moist juncture.

She gasped when he found it, and his hand came back around her belly to pull her into him even more, fingers long and searching, seeking and finding that spot. He surged upwards in one move and he was there, where she ached for him, thrusting deep. Rowan twisted back further and he came up on one arm, bending down and meeting her mouth with his. His kiss was gentle. The whole experience was so gentle it was breaking her heart. He was careful to stay away from the sore side of her mouth.

His head moved down. He was setting up a rhythm that was fast hurtling her towards nirvana, and when his mouth found one hard peak, thrusting forward flagrantly, and suckled fiercely, nirvana broke all around her, within her. She clutched his arm, his own tempo quickened, and with one last surge she felt him come deep inside her.

They lay like that for a long moment, Isandro pulling Rowan tight in against him, almost as if he wanted to fuse their bodies together. Eventually he pulled free and Rowan lay flat on her back. Isandro propped himself up beside her. She looked at him, still breathless. He just watched her. A fine sheen of sweat made her skin glow. She lifted a hand and traced his jaw. He took it and sucked a finger deep into his mouth.

A pulse throbbed between her legs. How could he have the power to arouse her so easily, so quickly? She knew her eyes had widened.

He frowned lightly. As he watched her expression something crept over him. Could it be possible?

'You...*this* frightens you, doesn't it? The way you are with me here, in bed...'

She just looked up at him, fear and confusion evident in her eyes. He didn't know how he hadn't seen it before. Too blinded by lust. By events.

She nodded slowly, and then said shakily, 'Terrified... I feel like I become someone else...someone I don't know...' She whispered the last words. 'And yet I need it, crave it, and that makes me feel...'

His mouth quirked slightly. 'Wanton? Lusty? Sexy? Sensual?'

Rowan grimaced. 'Well...some of those things.'

He moved over her then and let her feel the evidence of his own resurgence of arousal. He found her hand and brought it down, making her encircle his shaft, moving her hand up and down with his.

His voice sounded rough, hoarse. 'Sex is messy, guttural, wonderful and base...and all I know is I've never experienced it with anyone else the way I do with you. You are all those things, Rowan, and more...'

He took his hand away and rested over her on both forearms, his weight deliciously heavy against her. She kept her hand on him, moving up and down, and watched fascinated as passion glazed his eyes and tautened the skin across his cheekbones. Desire flooded her, but she only cared about giving him pleasure.

When his head went back and the muscles in his neck corded she knew he was close. He reached down and stopped her hand, coming close and pressing his mouth to hers, and then he filled her again. She gasped and arched upwards, wanting all of him, every inch. He started to move and, together again, they reached the blazing heights.

The following morning Rowan awoke to find Julia bustling into the room with breakfast on a tray. Her automatic impulse was to sit up, but then she realised she was naked. She pulled up the sheet quickly. Julia appeared not to notice anything unusual in finding Rowan in Isandro's bed.

She settled the tray beside Rowan and clucked around her like a mother hen, fluffing up the pillows. As she was leaving, Rowan asked her about Zac. Julia told her that Ana-Lucía had already fed him, and that he was downstairs with Isandro.

Rowan sank back. The breakfast looked appetizing, but her stomach lurched. A million things hit her brain at once. She'd spent the night in Isandro's bed. He hadn't left her. They'd made love. Or that was how it had felt. Her heart clenched. She was in so deep now that the thought of leaving again, this time through no choice of her own, was filling her with dread.

She heard a noise and the door opened. Isandro. Her mouth went dry and her cheeks flushed at the thought of last night.

His eyes went from her to the breakfast. 'Not hungry?'

Her mouth tightened as she watched him come in. 'Not really...' She couldn't read his expression. He seemed remote, different from the man who had taken her to heaven and back last night. Who had been so tender.

He stood at the window for a moment before turning around. 'Look, Rowan, about last night...I'm sorry...I never meant for...that to happen. When I offered to sleep with you I meant just that. Sleep.'

Rowan sat up straight, holding the sheet against her. White-hot pain blanked out the previous night and the urge to self-protect rose up swiftly. She rushed to halt any more words. 'Oh, no—please don't worry. I hadn't expected that either. It was just an effect of the day. The extreme circumstances.'

Her cheeks were crimson, and she looked with despair to where her robe was flung on a chair in the corner. He saw her look, and with a rigid jaw strolled over to get it.

All she wanted to do was get out of there and away from the pity he must feel. He'd been offering comfort; she'd taken complete liberties with that. Hadn't he made it tacitly clear after the other night that any desire for her had burnt itself out? Her role as his mistress had been laughably short in the end. But last night, she could almost have believed...

He handed her the robe. She glanced up quickly and saw his face was like granite. She sensed anger and felt bewildered. A knife skewered her heart. He regretted it that much? She'd have to make moves to leave the house soon if she couldn't even be trusted to control herself around him.

She grabbed the robe and pulled it on without managing to show a sliver of flesh. She stood up from the bed. 'I'll eat this downstairs…I'd like to see Zac anyway.'

He stopped her just before she went to lift the tray. 'Let me.'

Rowan felt even more exposed. He must have seen her hands shaking. He took it and walked out, and she followed miserably.

At the bottom of the stairs he turned to her, his eyes guarded. 'The police are due here in about an hour to take a statement from you. Are you up to it?'

Rowan's heart contracted. For all the world he sounded genuinely concerned. She nodded. 'Yes. I'll be fine.'

When she followed Isandro into the dining room after that she was immeasurably relieved to see Zac playing happily with Ana-Lucía, seemingly suffering no ill effects of the day before.

Isandro disappeared into his office after the police had been and gone. He'd sat by her side throughout the interview, and Rowan had felt his tension growing as she'd related the events. Undoubtedly he must blame her to some extent. How could he not?

After playing with Zac until his nap, Rowan retreated to the walled garden of the private patio outside her room. Under the shade of a huge tree she was trying to read, but gave up when she realised how futile it was. Her cheeks burned again, and her insides twisted in embarrassment when she thought of last night. What was going to happen now?

She would have to call that estate agent and see if he had found anything yet. One thing was clear: she needed to leave as soon as possible. No doubt Isandro would allow her a little grace, considering what had happened, but she couldn't take advantage of that. She was too volatile around him, barely able to control herself.

The divorce would most likely be through quickly— Isandro would want to be free to get on with his own life, possibly even remarry. The sooner she made the break, got some distance, the sooner she could start to claw back some control…get on with things. Rowan's fists clenched unconsciously in rejection of her thoughts.

She heard the shrill ring of her mobile phone from inside her room and hurried in to get it. Her heart thumped a little erratically as she realised exactly who it must be. Her past reached out ghostly tentacles to claim her, and she brushed off a feeling of foreboding.

As she'd expected, it was a call to remind her of her appointment. She hung up, and hugged her arms around herself, suddenly feeling cold. At that moment she wished she had someone to turn to, someone who would share her concerns, her worries. For a fleeting moment she wondered wistfully what it might be like to be loved, completely and deeply, by someone like Isandro…to be supported.

Just then a knock sounded at her door. She opened it, and the object of her thoughts and fantasies was standing there, looking grim. She clutched the door. No doubt this was it. He wanted to talk about the arrangements.

'Can you come down to my study? There's something I'd like to talk to you about.'

'Of course,' she said faintly, feeling sick.

In the study, Isandro told Rowan to sit down on the leather couch by the wall-to-ceiling shelves, but she shook her head minutely. 'If it's okay, I'd prefer to stand.'

He went and picked up a file from his desk and came to stand in front of her. A long moment stretched as he just looked at her, as if he was trying to figure her out, and Rowan's nerves screamed.

'How is your mouth?' he asked then, innocuously.

Rowan blinked and had to forcibly ignore an image of his

head coming towards her, and a kiss so light she almost hadn't felt it. She touched it gingerly. 'Fine…much better.'

Her hand dropped. 'What…what did you want to talk about?'

He glanced at the file in his hand and looked up, a harsh glitter in his eyes. He held it up. 'This is the result of the investigation I've had done into your whereabouts for the past two years.'

He knew? The thought set panic racing through her. This wasn't what she'd expected. She shook her head, as if to clear it. Had she heard right? 'I don't know what you're talking about… You investigated me?'

He nodded grimly. 'A little after the fact, I'll admit, but I didn't do it at the time because of extenuating circumstances: namely becoming a single parent, and shortly afterwards a stock market crash that threatened the livelihood of millions in Europe.'

The market crash that woman had mentioned at the party…

As if he had read her thoughts, he said, 'The crash that you appear to know nothing about.'

Rowan wanted to sink onto the couch behind her, but wouldn't. She wasn't sure she was ready for where this was inevitably headed, especially in light of her recent phone call. Feeling cowardly she played for time.

'I'm not sure I know where you're going with this.'

'Neither do I.' He tapped the file against an open hand. 'Do you want to know what my investigators found out?'

Rowan gave a little half-shrug and shook her head at the same time. No, she didn't want to see the facts of her life laid out in a file. Especially if—

'Here—have a look.'

He handed her the file, and with her heart palpitating in her chest Rowan opened it out. It was empty. Not one piece of paper. Relief mixed with something else raced through her.

He started to pace, and finally rested a hip against the edge of his desk, arms crossed formidably over his broad chest. He quirked a brow. 'I think I'm ready for your explanation, Rowan. Because unless you've been sitting on a mountain top in India meditating for two years, you haven't popped up anywhere in the world. And, believe me, we've searched.'

She could well imagine he had.

This was it. The moment of truth.

She carefully put down the file and went to stand by the window, looking outside for a long time, praying for courage. When she turned around Isandro was just watching her, his expression guarded, not a hint of warmth, *anything*. This was it. She had to tell him. He above anyone deserved to know.

'You haven't found any trace of me because when I walked out of the hospital that day I cut up all my cards, any trace of paperwork. I used my middle name, Louise, and my mother's maiden name, Miller. I moved my inheritance to a Swiss bank account and withdrew cash as I needed it.'

Rowan knew she was talking, and looking at Isandro as she did so, but she felt removed, as if she were watching herself from a long distance. She gripped the back of a chair that was in front of her.

'That still doesn't tell me where you've been. It just tells me how you evaded detection.' His voice was flat. Grim.

Rowan breathed and swallowed painfully, tried to say the words as dispassionately as possible. But she could feel her fingers digging into the chair-back. 'I was in France—a small town just outside Paris. I've been there since the day after I walked out of the hospital. In a clinic.'

She saw Isandro frown, and felt a cold sweat break out on her brow. She prayed for the fortitude to see this through. She closed her eyes for a second and opened them again. Took a deep breath.

'It was…is…a cancer clinic.'

CHAPTER ELEVEN

ISANDRO stood from the desk. Rowan felt shaky and light-headed, as if she was going to faint. She took deep breaths. He came close and gripped her upper arms, pulled her round to sit in the chair.

'Explain.'

Rowan looked up a long way and said weakly, 'Can you sit down, please? You're making me dizzy.'

He pulled up a chair and sat down opposite her, his whole body screaming tension. She focused on his eyes, which were a more intense blue than she'd ever seen before. She willed him to believe what she was about to say. She knew she wouldn't be able to bear it if he laughed or told her she was making up a story.

Shakily, she tucked some hair behind her ear. 'When I was seven months pregnant I went for a check-up. I'd been feeling more tired than usual…run down… I'd got a couple of colds…'

Isandro frowned, something flashing into his head. 'You had all those nosebleeds…'

Rowan nodded slightly, surprised that he remembered. At one point she'd been having two or three nosebleeds a week. 'That…they were a part of it too.'

Isandro looked at her. She *had* seemed more poorly in the

latter months of her pregnancy. He had put her increasing distance down to that. He nodded at her to continue, feeling curiously numbed, as if already protecting himself from something.

'Dr Campbell did a routine blood test and sent it to the lab. She called a couple of days later and asked me to come in and see her. You…you were meant to be going to New York for the week-long conference and you got delayed by a day.'

Isandro nodded again briefly. He could remember coming back from that trip and finding Rowan cool and distant. That had been the start of it. And he could also remember the pain of leaving that townhouse behind, the loneliness that would creep up on him during trips away, surprising him with its force…surprising him with its presence.

'When I went back to see Dr Campbell she had another doctor with her…' She took a deep breath. 'A visiting consultant haematologist, Professor Erol Villiers…' Rowan looked away for a moment and pressed her lips together before looking back. 'They told me that they'd found something in my blood. AML. It's an acute form of leukaemia.'

No matter how much she said it, or how quickly, the terror of that moment would always be with her.

She watched Isandro for his reaction, but he was unmoving, impassive. She recognised shock. Feeling claustrophobic, Rowan stood and walked back to the window, crossing her arms. It was easier to move, to not be so close, under such scrutiny.

'They wanted me to start an aggressive cycle of chemotherapy straight away, but I refused.' She heard Isandro stand behind her and turned around.

He was shaking his head. 'Why did you refuse?'

It was almost a relief to have him react. 'Because it could have harmed the baby. There was a risk of premature labour…malformity. There was no way I was going to put him at risk. I wouldn't do it then and I wouldn't do it now, if I had to choose again.'

'But…' Isandro turned away and paced back and forth. He couldn't even begin to articulate a coherent response. His brain, normally able to function at a level that left most people in the dust, now refused to operate.

'Just let me finish. I know…I know it's a lot.'

He stood facing her again, a raw intensity in his eyes.

'Because I refused to have the chemotherapy I knew I was severely reducing my chances of survival. But…' She shrugged. 'The most important thing was delivering Zac safely. That was all I cared about.'

'To the detriment of your own health?' He was incredulous.

Rowan nodded. 'And in case you're worried there was never any risk to Zac from my diagnosis. Not then, not now…'

Isandro looked grim, but Rowan continued. 'They wanted to start me on chemo straight after Zac was delivered, and I knew what was likely to be involved—how invasive it was going to be, how debilitating, with no guarantee of any success. Even so, Professor Villiers asked me to go to his specialist clinic in France. He was interested in my case as this type of cancer in pregnancy is rare.'

Rowan rubbed her hands up and down her arms. 'My own mother died of breast cancer when I was five. I remembered her treatment, the pain, the degradation… I didn't want to put Zac through bonding with me even for a short time, only to have me…taken away from him. I knew he'd be safe with you. You were so happy at the thought of a son…'

She reached out and held onto the back of the chair again like a lifeline.

'I meant it when I told you that I hadn't ever expected to

see you or Zac again. I truly didn't have any hope for the future. The doctors warned me that it would most likely have spread too far, too fast. Going to France was somewhere for me to go…to be…'

To die.

The unspoken words hung in the air.

'So what happened?' Isandro asked flatly.

Rowan knew that the last thing he'd have expected was to be faced with having to feel any kind of sympathy for her. So she made her words as clipped and impersonal as possible, hiding the acute pain of what she'd endured.

'They started me on the chemotherapy anyway, but as they had expected it didn't precipitate a remission. It was too late.' Self-consciously she touched her hair. 'This…my hair fell out. And the scar you noticed…it was from an intravenous line for fluids.'

Isandro was still unmoving. It made something contract protectively inside Rowan. But she went on. She had to.

'The only other possible option we hadn't explored was a bone marrow transplant. That's because it can't happen without a donor match. As all my close family were dead it was more or less ruled out, and time was running out…'

She crossed her arms tight across her chest, locked in the memories. 'But a few weeks after I arrived a perfect match became available within the clinic itself. It was from one of the registered voluntary bone marrow donors who happened to be related to a patient…however, it was going to be an extremely risky operation.'

'Why didn't you contact me then, if there was a chance?' Isandro's voice was unbearably harsh, and Rowan flinched slightly as it brought her back into the room. She looked at him unswervingly.

'Because even at this point there was only a fifty-fifty

hance. Less. You with all your money and influence could
ot have improved on that. And after a bone marrow transplant
ou're kept in isolation for up to a month, possibly longer,
ery prone to infections. Visitors are kept to a minimum.'

She paled. 'I contracted at least three infections. Even
f the transplant is successful, and you survive the infec-
ions, there's every chance the new marrow could be
ejected by the body months down the line. Don't you see?'
he beseeched him. 'What would have been the point?'
Ier voice cracked ominously but she forged ahead, 'I
adn't expected to survive that far, and I couldn't have
orne not being able to see Zac, being separated by two
oors in a quarantine area…'

Isandro stuck his hands deep in his jean pockets and then
ook them out again. His fists were clenched. Rowan looked
o vulnerable and defenceless standing behind the chair. A
urge of emotion broke through the awful numbness and in-
tinctively he moved towards her. But then abruptly he
topped again. He felt…he felt as if he was being torn in two.
Like nothing else he'd ever experienced. He wanted to go over
o her and crush her to him, hold her in his arms and never
et her go. And yet…much to his utter shame…he couldn't.
Not yet. Couldn't even hold her, because he was afraid of
vhat might erupt out of him if he did. Unbeknownst to him,
is face suddenly looked drawn and lined.

'And the note?'

Rowan flushed. 'That was to ensure you didn't come after
ne. I was hoping to dent your ego, your pride…'

She saw a flare of something in his eyes, but it died away,
ecause he had to acknowledge that she'd been right. And that
rked him beyond belief.

She looked down at her hands. 'I'd written other letters to
ou and to Zac. Letters to be sent…explaining everything.

Saying sorry. I wouldn't have wanted Zac to grow up thinking the worst of me.'

'Yet you've let me do that for nearly two months now?'

Her conscience struck her. She looked up again. Not telling him had been the only thing holding her fragile control together. 'I did try to tell you a couple of times…it wasn't the easiest subject to bring up. That day I bumped into you in London *was* literally my first day back from France. I truly had no idea that hotel was yours.' Her mouth twisted. 'It really was fate…circumstance.'

Isandro remembered his towering rage that day, remembered that she had indeed said something about wanting to explain. He remembered the other night, his cruel words, her reaction…but how could he have known *this*? He could feel himself retreating somewhere inside. That numbness was spreading through him again, and he welcomed it because it was removing him from *feeling*.

'I wanted to write you a letter through my solicitor and explain everything before we met, so that you might understand. That's why I was meeting Mr Fairclough.'

Isandro paced away and then back again. His brain finally seemed to click into gear. Every line in his body was rigid with tension. '*Why* didn't you tell me when you found out? For God's sake, I know it was just a marriage of convenience but you were carrying my child. I would have supported you no matter what. You shouldn't have had to go through that on your own.'

Rowan turned away from the anger in his voice, the censure. She still had to protect herself. 'I didn't tell you because I was afraid you'd side with the doctors and force me to have the chemo. I can't explain how I felt…all I know is that Zac's health and safety were paramount to me. I didn't want you to feel…*obliged* to care for me. To feel you had to do the right thing—which could have possibly harmed Zac but given me a better chance.'

She turned back and her eyes were defiant. 'I made a decision to deal with it on my own. To put Zac first and then deal with it myself.' Her voice didn't hold even a thread of self-pity. 'I've always been on my own, Isandro. It's what I'm used to. And I never…never expected to be here, explaining all of this to you.' Her voice shook with quiet intensity. 'I would *never* have walked away from Zac that day if I had believed there might be a chance…you *have* to believe me.'

He did. He did believe her. The pain was etched on her face even now. In her eyes. It was the pain he'd glimpsed before. That urge to take her in his arms almost overwhelmed him with its force, but was crushed down by the weight of guilt, heavy and pervasive.

When his investigators had turned up precisely nothing on Rowan's whereabouts he knew something had happened. This had been compounded by her behaviour since they'd met again in London. Her obvious devotion to Zac, her love for him. He hadn't mistaken the emotion she'd shown around him those first few days, weeks. When he'd thought it had been an act.

He realised now how overwhelming it must have been for her, her intention to live nearby…he couldn't ignore the facts any longer. She just wasn't the person who had left that callous and flippant note.

But what did this mean?

His head reeled. More than reeled. It was spinning off into space with all these facts. He was beginning to feel so many things that he had to keep a lid on his emotions. He took refuge in attack, hating himself because he knew well it was directed at the wrong person, but he was unable to stop. He asked ascerbically, 'Did you not think I'd support you?'

She was white as snow, her eyes two huge pools of violet

in her face. The gash on her lip was stark, and made some
thing clench in his chest, his heart.

'Of course I knew you'd support me, Isandro. But ou
marriage wasn't ever about that. I...couldn't face the though
of...dutiful support. You hadn't signed up for that.'

A maelstrom seemed to erupt inside Isandro. He hadn'
signed up for the passionate chemistry that had explode
between them either. Hadn't signed up for the way she'
turned his life upside down in so many ways. *Was* turning i
upside down. His voice was icy. '*That's* how you could justif
leaving?' He knew he sounded harsh, remote, but he couldn'
help it. Something was weighing him down inside.

A bleakness filled Rowan's heart and soul. He didn'
understand. He'd never understand. How could he? And in th
face of this cold front she knew she was still a coward. Sh
had left that day for myriad reasons, not least of which ha
been Zac and his welfare. But also because she had love
Isandro too much. To see him shackled to her for the days
weeks, possibly months on end...to witness his pity...to hav
him witness her downward slide...his responsibility for he
had been too much to bear. A painful ache lodged in he
throat.

She looked away and then back. Her voice was so quiet h
almost didn't hear her.

'I overheard your conversation with Ana. So you don'
have to explain anything to me. I knew exactly where I stood.

Isandro's head was beginning to hurt. 'My conversatio
with Ana...?'

Rowan crossed her arms. 'It was the day I'd found ou
about my prognosis...' She balked for a second. At the tim
she had intended telling him everything—until she'd over
heard... She gulped and forced her mind away from it. 'An
was angry.'

And then he *did* remember. Vividly. The way his sister had tried to back him into a corner, make him reveal himself when he hadn't even known how he felt. All he had known was that he'd wanted to protect Rowan from Ana's vitriol, which stemmed from his father's betrayal of them all.

'I hadn't meant to listen. I came home from meeting Dr Campbell and heard you…' She lifted a hand ineffectually and let it drop. 'You didn't say anything I wasn't already aware of.' She prayed he wouldn't see how badly she was lying.

The words came back to haunt him now. Clearly Rowan had heard the worst of it. Like shards of crystal, moments, snippets started to come to Isandro. The timing of when she'd withdrawn into herself, cut herself off from him emotionally and physically… But he couldn't grasp the implications of it all fully—not yet.

Her voice didn't ring with the conviction it had when she'd told him of her illness. In fact she seemed all too brittle now. He felt that brittleness spread through him too. The world was reduced to that room and he couldn't *feel* anything. It was all too huge to take in, too abstract. To have believed one thing for so long…and now this.

Rowan stood still, looking at a spot in the carpet for so long that she was beginning to feel dizzy. Then Isandro finally spoke, and Rowan looked at him reluctantly, afraid to see what might be in his eyes. But she couldn't read their expression, they were veiled.

'So…what now?'

What now indeed?

She almost welcomed the banality of words. Even though they were really far from banal. 'I have to go back to the clinic for a couple of days. I've been in remission now for some months, but Professor Villiers wants to see me for a routine check-up just to confirm that everything is okay.'

'When?'

'Tomorrow.'

'That's not much notice.'

Rowan's heart ached at Isandro's astringent tone. 'They believe me to be in London, I was going to take the train. And in truth I'd forgotten about it…with everything.' She flushed.

'You can take the plane.'

Rowan looked at him, slightly aghast at his easy offer. 'Well, I…thank you. I'd appreciate that.'

And just like that it was out. Her big terrible dark secret. And nothing had changed. They were right where they'd always been. In some kind of no man's land.

Isandro's phone rang on his desk, making Rowan flinch. He looked at her for a long moment, and then with an impatient gesture went to answer it. Rowan slipped quietly out of the room.

CHAPTER TWELVE

Two Days Later

'I CAN'T stress enough how ill your wife was, Mr Salazar. The fact that she survived at all is a testament to her strength, and the sheer luck of finding that donor when we did. She showed great courage in the face of daily pain on a level that you or I can only imagine.'

The stark words struck deep. He looked at Rowan's doctor. Isandro had arrived early that morning. When Rowan had left early the previous day he hadn't even accompanied her to the plane, unable to break out of the stasis that had gripped him since she'd told him everything. Since then his mind, his heart, had been a seething mass of pain, anger, confusion. And something else.

'Professor Villiers, I know I wasn't here…when my wife was going through her treatment—'

The doctor waved a hand. 'It's none of my business, but I knew she'd decided to go it alone for her own reasons, which is why we could never tell you. As you know, doctor-patient confidentiality is sacrosanct. As the symptoms of her illness were largely *a*symptomatic, her pregnancy disguised them. She got away with not telling you.'

He took off his spectacles and looked slightly fierce. 'I won't lie to you, though. There were times when I wished she wasn't so stubborn. She wouldn't even let us induce the baby early. She wanted to give him the best possible chance—and that, of course, reduced her own chances even more…'

Isandro reeled anew. And took a deep breath. Enough. 'I need to know. I have to know what she went through… *please*.'

The doctor looked at Isandro for a long moment and then, as if he'd seen something he could trust, he nodded briefly.

'Very well.'

Relief surged through Isandro. Professor Villiers stood up.

'Of course I can't reveal any of Rowan's specific details without her permission, but I can tell you what someone in her position might have gone through.'

'Thank you.' Isandro stood when the doctor gestured to the door.

'Come, we will walk and talk. Have you seen your wife yet?'

Isandro shook his head.

'Then I will take you to her when we're done.'

Isandro stood leaning against the open doors that led outside to a pretty garden area. It was a sunny day and patients and visitors strolled the paths.

But he didn't see that.

He saw images: the room where Rowan had had to be on her own for almost three months as she battled infections after the transplant. The equipment she'd been hooked up to.

His hands were deep in his pockets, clenched tight against the pain inside him. The pain of how close he'd come to—

And then there she was. She looked so healthy now, so vibrant, it made it hard to believe… He stepped out and walked towards her. She was sitting cross-legged with a group of children around her. She was reading a story and looked about sixteen herself, in a flowery summer dress. Bare legs, bare feet.

He sat on a bench and just watched. Drinking her in, trying to come to terms with so much. And he thought that perhaps now he understood a little.

Rowan finished the story and looked up with a smile—only to look straight into Isandro's piercing blue eyes. It was as if they'd been drawn there like a magnet. He was sitting on a bench just feet away, watching her. The breath stalled in her throat, and she could feel the colour drain from her face. Perhaps she was dreaming, because in this very spot so many times she'd fantasised... Absently, she hugged and kissed the children.

She stood awkwardly and slipped her sandals back on. Isandro stood up as she approached. He was real, not a figment of her imagination. She tried to ignore the fluttering in her chest, the aching in her heart, and called up the very real need to protect herself.

'Isandro...what are you doing here?' She sounded breathless and cursed herself.

He looked down at her and she could see his eyes flash, something swirling in their depths. 'I think I owe you this at least. I should have come with you yesterday, not let you go on your own.'

'Oh...it's fine, really. I hadn't expected it.'

A pain lanced him. He took her hand in his and looked at it almost absently. 'No, I don't suppose you did.' He looked up and gestured to where she'd been sitting with the children. 'Who are they?'

Rowan wanted to pull her hand away. She was feeling hot and bothered. And confused. 'They're...they're patients.' She had to concentrate. 'When it was finally confirmed that I was in remission three months ago I was still weak. I had to build up my strength, so I helped out with the kids...' She shrugged then, and looked down. 'I always feel so guilty for getting well again, when they should have their whole lives ahead of them.'

'It's nothing to feel guilty about.' Isandro said with a quiet fierceness that surprised her.

'Yes.' She said simply, still shocked to see him here. And then she said the words she'd thought she'd never say. 'The results are good; I'm still in remission and I'm getting stronger.' She took a deep breath. 'My prognosis is…very good.'

She searched his face but couldn't fathom what was going on in his head. It must be pity. She hardened her heart. And then he took the wind out of her sails again by asking, 'Show me the new wing they're building?'

Her mouth opened and closed. 'Dr Villiers told you?'

He nodded.

Rowan led the way, and when Isandro reached for her hand she let him take it. What was the harm? Soon enough they'd be discussing the divorce, custody… If he was doing this out of pity then she'd be a coward and take it.

They approached a building site around the back of the clinic where a makeshift wooden plaque hung on the fence. It read: *The Catherine and Alistair Carmichael Wing for the research and treatment of children's leukaemia.*

Isandro's voice sounded tight. 'Why did you use your parents' names?'

He felt Rowan shrug, and she touched the plaque briefly with a finger. 'So they can live on together…through this.'

Isandro's head reeled with her selflessness. 'All your inheritance?'

Rowan looked up at him then, and shook her head. 'Not all. I kept some back for legal fees in case…in case…' She avoided his eye and couldn't finish, but it was hard, his gaze was so penetrating, 'I knew you'd most likely pursue a divorce…I expected that.'

His eyes were too intense. She had to look away. The pain was debilitating. She pulled her hand from his and started to walk. Her emotions were threatening to erupt again. To be here, sharing this with him, was too much.

Rowan packed up her few things and said goodbye to the staff and Dr Villiers, who gave her a huge bear hug. Isandro was waiting for her.

In the car Rowan sat as far apart from him as possible. She felt as if he'd looked inside her brain, her heart.

Just when she saw that they were passing the sign for the airport, she heard him say, 'I've booked us into a hotel in Paris for the night.'

She looked over, aghast. 'Why?'

He was looking at her with an expression she couldn't decipher and she didn't like the determination in his eyes.

'Isandro, you don't have to do this. Please. I'm not a child who's just had a nasty trip to the dentist. I'd much prefer to go home.' *Not that his home was her home.*

His jaw clenched ominously. 'I'd like to take you out for the evening. We have to talk, Rowan. It might as well be here as Seville.'

Was he afraid that she mightn't be able to take the news well? Did he see her as somehow delicate now that he knew? Didn't he know how prepared she was? *Who was she kidding…?* She looked out of the window and could see that already they were on the motorway, headed for the centre of Paris. She shrugged. He was right. It might as well be here as in Spain.

They pulled up outside the Four Seasons Georges V Hotel, one of the most exclusive in Paris. Rowan felt severely under-dressed in her flowery dress. Isandro came around the car and took her by the hand, further unsettling her, and led her inside.

He was greeted obsequiously by the staff. Rowan was amused to see that for someone like Isandro checking in wasn't expected. A senior member of staff greeted him immediately and ushered them into a lift, taking them straight up to their room. Her head was spinning as they were led in and she looked around. Opulent didn't even come into it.

She wandered around while Isandro dealt with the manager. Ornate doors led out onto a private patio, with a stunning private view onto the Eiffel Tower. It was early evening by now, and the distinctive shape of the tower was set against a beautiful clear sky streaked with mauve.

Rowan went and leaned on the railing, barely noticing the table set for two. She assumed that it came with the room as standard—after all, she thought cynically, wasn't Paris the most romantic city in the world? And this one of its finest hotels? That brought her up short. What did Isandro expect? Why was he doing this? Were duty and pity fuelling these actions?

She turned quickly to find him standing in the doorway, watching her. She couldn't read the expression on his face. But it was *intent*. And it made her heart flip-flop. She had to stop this now, get a hold of herself. She was way too vulnerable after the trip to the clinic.

'Isandro…this is lovely…but crazy. Surely you haven't brought us here for some kind of…?'

His mouth twisted into a grim line. 'Romantic evening?'

She coloured. Her throat felt tight. He strolled towards her and she had nowhere to go. She had to stop him.

'Exactly. It's nice to be here, but you could have booked somewhere more…modest—two rooms…'

The bed loomed large in the background. Her heart thudded so loud that she felt sure he must hear it.

'What if I do want this, Rowan? What if I want all of this?'

She frowned. 'I don't know what you mean.'

He was so close now that all she would have to do was reach out and pull him to her. She looked up. And wished she didn't have to look into his eyes.

'Take a look around. Don't you know where we are yet?'

She shook her head, feeling seriously confused. He took her hand and led her back into the room. Suddenly it *was* clear. The room was so sensually decorative...so romantic. A bottle of champagne peeped out from an ice bucket on a nearby table, two crystal flutes beside it sparkled. She gasped, and her hand tightened reflexively around his.

'It's the honeymoon suite.' She felt sick. What kind of joke was this?

He turned her around to face him, his hands on her shoulders.

Anger surged. 'Sandro, I don't know what this is all for, but you can ring down right now and tell them we're not staying here. I don't know what you think—'

She broke free. He couldn't know, could he? Had she been so transparent? Frantically she tried to deny her feelings, deny that he might have read them.

'We do have to talk, Isandro—but does it have to be here? I mean, isn't this some sort of mockery?'

'You think that wanting to make a new start is mockery?' His voice was frigid.

Rowan looked at him in bewilderment. 'What new start? We're getting divorced. I'm moving out.'

'I've stopped divorce proceedings.'

Her jaw dropped and her heart stopped. 'You've *what*? Why?' she asked a little wildly.

'I think it's obvious now that we should stay married. There's Zac. And your safety to consider.'

Rowan felt cornered, trapped. 'So in effect nothing will have changed? It'll still be a marriage of convenience, only now you know what happened, so you can forgive me for my past sins, I'll be allowed to be a mother to Zac, and you can keep us safe if we're all together.'

'Is that so bad a prospect?' he asked quietly, a different quality in his voice.

'No...*yes!*' Rowan threw her hands up in the air. He didn't know what he was asking. It was heaven and hell. Her heart was pumping so hard that it threatened to burst from her chest. She looked at him and begged him silently to understand, not to do this.

'Isandro, I can't. I won't. It's not fair on me or you or Zac. He deserves to have two parents who love one another, and I won't stand by and watch you sacrifice your happiness just out of a sense of pity and duty. We can live a perfectly happy life divorced. I can live nearby, see Zac...'

'*No.* I won't have that.'

Rowan blanched at the vehemence in his voice.

He came and pulled her over to a silk-covered sofa, sitting her down. She could feel the tension in his body transmitting into her own. She ached for him even now, body and soul.

She opened her mouth to speak, but he got in first. 'Rowan, just...let me speak, okay?'

She nodded warily. His hands were on hers, heavy.

'Professor Villiers showed me around today, and without going into the details of your case told me what you would have gone through. I saw the quarantine room...he told me about the treatments... That was why you had the bad dreams, wasn't it?'

Rowan closed her eyes weakly. It was all coming back. 'Don't...'

'I won't. But...'

She opened her eyes again, and the pain in them nearly stopped Isandro—but he had to keep going. 'It nearly destroyed me to see what you had to endure, Rowan. No one should have to feel they have no option but to endure that alone. And I'm sorry—I'm so sorry that you felt that was your only option.'

Rowan shook her head. 'You really don't have to do all this just because—'

'I'm not. You made your own choices. I wish you'd included me, but I think I can see now why you didn't. I couldn't take it in when you told me first. I had no real concept of what you faced until today…'

That made her sit up. She looked into his eyes. He was sincere.

'When we got married I was away a lot. Too much I can see now. I saw it at the time too…but you were never meant to get in the way of my business. I didn't know why I was suddenly feeling…wanting…' He stopped ineffectually. 'We had no time to get to know one another properly. You got pregnant so quickly.'

'Which never should have happened.'

He shook his head emphatically. 'It would have happened sooner or later, Rowan. The truth is I desired you from the moment I saw you. I just hid it under very elaborate plans to marry you to further my career in Europe. I had an agenda and nothing was getting in my way. You see, I'd never planned on marrying for love or desire, after seeing what it did to my parents. When my sister and I were in our teens my father was driving home one night. He and my mother were having one of their passionate arguments and he crashed the car, leaving her paralysed from the waist down.'

An image of the tiny woman dressed in black in a wheelchair at their wedding came into Rowan's mind. The bitterness etched into her face. Isandro's voice dragged her attention back.

'My father was so racked with guilt for ruining his wife's

life that he took an English mistress and broke my mother's heart. And my sister's. That's the root of her own unhappiness at our union. But in truth I think she would have been unhappy with anyone I chose to marry. When my father failed her so badly, she put me on a pedestal instead.'

Rowan was feeling unsteady. This conversation was going into unknown territory that she wasn't prepared for. He had desired her all along? She tried to focus.

'When I saw you across that room and then found out you were Carmichael's daughter. I told myself the desire I felt was for power, pure and simple.' He shook his head, his eyes burning into hers. 'But that night, our wedding night, when we slept together that first time…'

Rowan blushed and looked away. She'd practically thrown herself at him. He guessed what she was thinking and put a hand to her chin, bringing her round to face him, 'No. It was mutual. I don't take women to bed out of pity, Rowan. And I don't keep taking them to bed unless I desire them.'

Her heart stopped.

'I…I always thought… And then when I was so…' She was blushing so hard now that her cheeks were literally burning.

Isandro rubbed the back of a hand across one hot surface. 'It was like that for me too. But then when you retreated into your shell…which I know now was after you'd been to the doctor…'

Rowan fought to stay sane despite the heated intensity in his eyes. He was guessing, *knowing* too much, nearly everything. She had to remind him before she duped herself into believing she was reading something in his eyes.

'But there was that conversation.'

His eyes didn't change; they blazed harder. 'Which was a mistake that you shouldn't have had to overhear. My sister was demanding to know how I felt about you. She's poisonous in her anger and her hatred of our father. If I had told her that I had feelings for you, she'd have gone out there and annihilated you. And, apart from that noble desire, I was an abject and miserable coward.'

Rowan frowned slightly.

'I was so confused about how I *was* feeling that I wasn't in any shape to articulate that to Ana.'

Feelings? He just meant friendship…warmth…respect.

Rowan felt as if she had to say something to avoid the awful moment when he would confirm that. 'Look, Sandro…I like you too. I liked you from the start. I had no choice but to marry you…my father…the bank. My inheritance.' *She had to convince him.*

He shook his head and sent up a silent plea. 'I don't believe you.' He held her hands even tighter.

Rowan's skin prickled and her belly fell. He wasn't going to do this to her, was he?

'Sandro, please…' she begged, trying to pull her hands away from his. 'I don't know what you want to hear.'

'You're a strong woman, Rowan. I think you've more than proved that you don't do anything you don't feel passionately about. And your inheritance? I don't think that's ever really mattered a damn. All I want to hear is the truth…'

The truth.

She shook her head helplessly, and to her chagrin her eyes filled with hopeless tears. 'You know. You *know*. That's why you're doing this…to make me agree…but I can't, Sandro. I can't.'

The blue of his eyes was hypnotic. 'Tell me,' he demanded hoarsely, not giving her an inch to back away.

And then the fight was too much. She was too tired. Did she really have the strength to walk away from a lifetime with Isandro even if he didn't love her? She knew the answer…

Her hands lay limp in his, and she looked to a spot over his shoulder. Anything to avoid the laser-like gaze. 'If I hadn't got sick I never would have left. I would have hoped and dreamt that some day you'd come to feel about me the way I felt for you.' She looked at him then, her eyes clear and true. 'I think I've loved you since our wedding night. I told myself I didn't love you any more when I saw you in London, but I knew I did. I was just trying to protect myself.'

She steeled herself. 'And I do now.' She shrugged one shoulder then, in an endearingly vulnerable gesture. 'You and Zac. My deepest most secret dream through all those months was of us as a family together…healthy and happy.'

Isandro took up her hands, and Rowan was surprised to feel his own hands shaking violently. He bent and pressed a kiss to her palms. *'Gracias, mi querida…'* He pressed another kiss to her hands, the other side. *'Mi vida…'*

Rowan still felt slightly shell shocked at what she'd just said. The urge to self-protect was still strong. Her back was still tense. 'Sandro…'

He lifted his head and he was smiling, grinning inanely. She'd never seen him look so happy. 'Rowan…*querida*…I fell in love with you too along the way. Somewhere you crept into my heart. When you gave birth to Zac—in that moment…I knew it then.'

A shadow crossed his face. He sobered. Rowan was holding her breath. Surely he wouldn't go *this* far just to get her to comply?

'When I came back and found you gone…found that note…'

He looked so bleak for a moment that Rowan had to believe. Tentative wings of joy started to take off in her heart.

'You were right. I was so angry, so incensed, that I damned you to hell and told myself I'd been the biggest fool. But the hurt didn't go. It festered. I told myself I'd been stupid to trust you when all along you'd turned out to be the same as every other money-hungry social climbing…' He stopped. 'That day when you walked away you didn't just walk out on Zac…you walked out on me, and I didn't think I could ever forgive you for it.'

Rowan's whole body and head were going into meltdown. 'I had no idea I meant anything to you at all. It was that that gave me the courage to go. I didn't want to burden you with a terminally ill wife you felt nothing for. I wanted you to be free to remarry…someone you loved and desired. And I couldn't bear for Zac to know the pain of separation…'

His hand came and cupped her jaw, his thumb catching a tear that she hadn't even been aware of. 'You're the only one, Rowan. I love and desire you, no one else. The other night…I know you read me wrong in the morning. I never meant that I didn't *want* to make love to you. I felt like a crass schoolboy when I should have been offering you nothing but comfort…yet I couldn't help myself. I haven't even been with another woman since you left. I couldn't. I told myself it was anger hampering me. I couldn't even go looking for you…the hurt was too intense.'

'Oh, my love…' Rowan's heart overflowed. If she was dreaming then she never wanted to wake up. She pressed a kiss to his palm and, unable to hold back any more, Isandro pulled her forward and crushed her against his chest.

'I love you, Rowan. You're my life.' He smiled ruefully for a second. 'I called you my mistress…that thought lasted about two minutes. I just couldn't see you like that, no matter how much I tried to distance myself.' He was serious again. 'When you and Zac were taken…when I saw you in that awful room…'

A shudder ran through his big frame, and Rowan welcomed him when his head bent and his mouth met hers in a searing kiss.

When they broke apart Rowan was crying in earnest. 'I'm so sorry I didn't tell you straight away…I just…couldn't…'

'Shh.' He kissed her again, pulling her close. 'It doesn't matter now. You're here, you're well, you're going to be well. Zac is well. We're together, and that's all that matters.'

Rowan nodded tearily.

Isandro gestured with a shoulder and sent a quick glance around the room. 'I brought you here because I want this to be a new start. We never had a honeymoon.'

Rowan shook her head in acknowledgment.

Isandro kissed her hand again. 'Well, now we will. Starting tonight. With dinner overlooking the Eiffel Tower.' He smiled a little ruefully, almost shyly, and it made Rowan's heart soar even higher. 'I know it's a bit of a cliché, the table overlooking the Eiffel Tower…the room…the champagne… I have so much catching up to do with you, Rowan. This is just the start of it…I promise.'

She shook her head vaguely, too entranced by his eyes and his words to be able to begin to tell him that it was all okay. Fine. Perfect. His words were washing over her like a healing balm.

And then he reached into a pocket and took something out. She looked down. In his palm he held her wedding and engagement rings. She watched wordlessly as he took her hand and slipped them onto her ring finger one by one. He'd had them resized and now they fitted perfectly.

Rowan reached up to touch his mouth with a finger, her eyes dropping in an innocently provocative gesture before looking back up. Her hand shook with the emotions running through her. 'You were so sure?'

He shook his head then, that vulnerable light still in his eyes, and caught her finger and kissed it. 'No, I wasn't sure at all…but I prayed to every god I know that you felt something for me…that you would at least agree to stay married.'

They shared a long intense look.

'Do you know what day tomorrow is?'

'Of course I do. It's Zac's birthday,' Rowan said huskily.

He smiled. 'So tomorrow, early, we go home, we wake up our son, and we give him a very special birthday—the first of many, *together*.'

Rowan smiled a wobbly smile. She was sure she must look a sight, but with Isandro gazing at her as if she were the Venus de Milo she didn't care. She let him take her hand, pull her up and lead her out to the terrace.

In the warm spring air of a beautiful night in Paris, they started again…

Four years later.

Rowan looked down in wonder at the small head full of dark auburn hair nestled against her breast. Watched the tiny puckered frown, the rosebud mouth suckling fiercely as if her life depended on it. A small hand curled around her little finger with a strength that was truly unbelievable. Her daughter. Alégria. *Joy*. Because that was what her pregnancy had been. One of hope and joy. There had been every chance that after the chemotherapy her fertility might have been irreparably damaged, but Alégria was proof otherwise.

The door opened with a burst, and a flash of blond barrelled in, followed by Isandro, tall and so handsome that Rowan smiled and her heart clenched as it always did. They shared a look, and then she turned her smiling attention to Zac as he clambered up onto the bed.

'Mamá, mamá—look what I drew for Légria!'

'It's *Alégria* sweetie…'

Zac clearly wasn't interested and chattered on, showing Rowan a drawing of Papá, Mamá, Zac and the new baby. Tears filled Rowan's eyes and Isandro saw them. He came and pressed a lingering kiss to her mouth. She just looked at him mutely, with everything written on her face, in her eyes. The moment was huge. Love blazed between them, strong and true.

Isandro just smiled at her. 'I know, *querida*…I know…'

researching the cure

The facts you need to know:

- Breast cancer is the most common form of cancer in the United Kingdom. **One woman in nine** will be affected by the disease in her lifetime.

- Every year over **44,000** women, **300** men are diagnosed with breast cancer and around **12,500** women and approximately **100** men will die from the disease.

- 80% of all breast cancers occur in post-menopausal women and approximately 8,800 pre-menopausal women are diagnosed with the disease each year.

- However, the five year survival rate has significantly improved, on average today 80% of women diagnosed with the disease will still be alive five years later, compared to 52% thirty years ago.

Breast Cancer Campaign's mission is to beat breast cancer by funding innovative world-class research to understand how breast cancer develops, leading to improved diagnosis, treatment, prevention and cure.

4 FREE

BOOKS AND A SURPRISE GIFT!

We would like to take this opportunity to thank you for reading this Mills & Boon® book by offering you the chance to take FOUR more specially selected titles from the Modern™ series absolutely FREE! We're also making this offer to introduce you to the benefits of the Mills & Boon® Book Club—

★ **FREE home delivery**
★ **FREE gifts and competitions**
★ **FREE monthly Newsletter**
★ **Exclusive Mills & Boon® Book Club offers**
★ **Books available before they're in the shops**

Accepting these FREE books and gift places you under no obligation to buy, you may cancel at any time, even after receiving your free shipment. Simply complete your details below and return the entire page to the address below. You don't even need a stamp!

YES! Please send me 4 free Modern books and a surprise gift. I understand that unless you hear from me, I will receive 6 superb new titles every month for just £2.99 each, postage and packing free. I am under no obligation to purchase any books and may cancel my subscription at any time. The free books and gift will be mine to keep in any case.

P8ZED

Ms/Mrs/Miss/Mr ....Initials ....
BLOCK CAPITALS PLEASE

Surname ....

Address ....

....

....Postcode.........................

Send this whole page to:
UK: FREEPOST CN81, Croydon, CR9 3WZ